Southern Rites

A MAX PORTER PARANORMAL MYSTERY

Stuart Jaffe

Southern Rites is a work of fiction. Names, characters, places, and incidents either are the product of the author's imagination or are used fictitiously, and any resemblance to any persons, living or dead, business establishments, events, or locales is entirely coincidental.

SOUTHERN RITES

Cover art by Claudia Ianniciello

ISBN 13: 978-1-963517-00-2

First Edition: October, 2016
First Hardcover Edition: February, 2024

For my bandmates,
Tim, Gary, and Tony

Also by Stuart Jaffe

Max Porter Paranormal Mysteries

Southern Bound
Southern Charm
Southern Belle
Southern Gothic
Southern Haunts
Southern Curses
Southern Rites
Southern Craft
Southern Spirit
Southern Flames
Southern Fury
Southern Souls
Southern Blood
Southern Graves
Southern Dead
Southern Hexes
Southern Hart

Nathan K Thrillers

Immortal Killers
Killing Machine
The Cardinal
Yukon Massacre
The First Battle
Immortal Darkness
A Spy for Eternity
Prisoner
Desert Takedown
Lone Star Standoff
The Puppeteer
Blowback
Prime

The Ridnight Mysteries

The Water Blade
The Waters of Taladoro
Waterfire

The Parallel Society

The Infinity Caverns
Book on the Isle
Rift Angel
Lost Time
Pages of Glass
The Bold Warrior
City of Infinity

The Malja Chronicles

The Way of the Black Beast
The Way of the Sword and Gun
The Way of the Brother Gods
The Way of the Blade
The Way of the Power
The Way of the Soul

Gillian Boone novels

A Glimpse of Her Soul
Pathway to Spirit

Stand Alone Novels

After The Crash
Real Magic
Founders

Short Story Collection

10 Bits of My Brain
10 More Bits of My Brain
The Bluesman
The Marshall Drummond Case Files: Cabinet 1
The Marshall Drummond Case Files: Cabinet 2
The Marshall Drummond Case Files: Cabinet 3

Non-Fiction

How to Write Magical Words: A Writer's Companion
For more information, please visit ***www.stuartjaffe.com***

Southern Rites

Chapter 1

ON SEVERAL OCCASIONS during Max Porter's youth, he heard his name called over the loudspeaker at school, summoning him to the principal's office. After enduring a raised eyebrow from the teacher and the hushed curiosity of his peers, Max walked the long hall which only seemed to stretch further away the more he walked. He had no idea if the news that waited would be good or bad, only that he dreaded the discovery. Walking up the driveway of a suburban Winston-Salem home, Max felt that way again.

His wife, Sandra, came up beside him on the right. They had been through a lot together — especially in recent days — and she had never wavered. He clasped her hand for a little extra strength.

"I don't like this," a rich voice said before Marshall Drummond appeared on Max's left side. Drummond, the ghost of a 1940s detective, had been a crucial partner in the Porter Agency since its inception. If Max had not already been feeling uneasy, this simple statement would have chilled his skin.

Sandra pointed out a realtor's FOR SALE sign. A large red SOLD had been slapped across the sign. Despite the hot weather, close to a month without rain, the lawn grew thick and green. Somebody had no qualms about conserving water.

"I'm telling you," Drummond went on, "this is a bad idea. You should both know by now that messing with witches never goes well."

"What should we do then?" Max said, unable to hide the growl in his voice. "It's been what? Three weeks since all that went down at the Devil's Tramping Ground? With the Hull family decimated, I figured we'd have had more time before this nonsense started up again. But Mother Hope and her Magi group call the shots now. And since she's a witch, we've got to deal with her. At least, until we can change things."

"Doesn't mean we've got to like it. We certainly don't have to come running like eager puppies."

"Well, I didn't expect to be hearing from them so soon. So excuse me if I'm a little off my game."

Sandra put out her hand. "Both of you — stop it. There's no need to be bickering. We've got to be calm and professional going in to whatever this is."

Max knew Sandra was right, but that didn't make it any easier to swallow. The call that came in that morning had made it clear — the Porter Agency, the research firm he and Sandra had built up with Drummond, now belonged to the Magi group. They could pretend that they were merely on retainer, but they all knew that the Magi group would never let it remain so simple.

As they walked across a red brick pathway, Max caught Drummond peeking in his coat pocket. That pocket was once the home of their friend Leed — a man who had died and been reduced to a ball of energy. The events that helped Mother Hope and the Magi gain power had also ripped Leed from the world. Other than an occasional glance at his pocket, Drummond had displayed no behavior of loss or mourning. Max could only hope his friend would be okay.

The front door opened and Leon Moore stepped out. Mother Hope's right-hand man, he stood tall and strong, his dark skin hiding his features in the soft shade of the porch. Max tightened his grip on Sandra's hand.

"Thank you for coming so fast," Leon said.

Max's top lip curled. "Didn't have a choice, did we?"

With a nod toward Sandra, Leon said, "You all look well. I'm glad to see nobody suffered too greatly from before."

Sandra's eyes flared. "You don't think a young boy being shot should be considered suffering?" The Sandwich Boys, PB and J, had been working for Max and Sandra only a short time, but PB took a bullet to the shoulder on their last case. "You call us from his bedside to do what? Check out an empty house for ghosts or something? Why bother with us? I'm just a beginner in witchcraft. Mother Hope has enough power of her own to handle whatever this is. Or perhaps we can lay out the truth — you really just want to show us who the boss is now. Isn't that right?"

With a confused grin, Leon stepped back to allow them inside. Max whispered to Sandra, "Way to keep it calm." As they passed Leon, Max eyed the man. "Looks like your witch boss is making you younger again."

Leon unconsciously rubbed his back. When Max had first met the man, he was an old librarian, stooped and weak. Since rising in power amongst the Magi, Leon had lost all of that. He still had gray in his hair and wrinkles on his skin, but Max knew that should the man be willing to make a deal, Mother Hope would be willing to cast a spell and shave off more years.

"Follow me, please," Leon said, and led the way deeper into the house.

Devoid of any furnishings, the empty house had a soft layer of dust on the wood flooring. Drummond floated nearby. "Looks like this place was on the market for quite some time."

Max knew Leon could not hear or see Drummond, but he still had to quell his natural reaction to shush the detective. He often wondered how Sandra dealt with it all — Max could only see and hear Drummond; Sandra saw and heard all ghosts.

As they headed single-file down a narrow hall, Leon said, "As part of the Restructuring, the Magi are purchasing several properties in Winston-Salem."

"The Restructuring?" Max asked.

"The Hull family controlled all of the magic usage in this state for so long, nobody really knows how to go forth now that they're gone. Since we're the only qualified group, and we are in charge at the moment, Mother Hope thought it was a good time to restructure the way things are to be done."

"And you need to buy property for that?"

Leon stopped at a closed door. "We need offices and housing for new employees and safe locations for those in trouble, not to mention prisons for those who break the law but are beyond the capabilities of the local police. It's quite a logistical endeavor. Then, of course, we want to protect the public from any houses that exude excessive magical energy."

"I don't know why I bothered asking. How about you open that door and get this show going? We really don't want to be here any longer than necessary."

Leon's nostrils flared, but otherwise he remained stoic. "Of course." He turned the knob and pushed open the door.

As Max entered the master bedroom, his skin prickled. The wooden floor had shattered toward the ceiling as if a giant fist had punched through from below. Many splintered boards stood perpendicular to the floor and some bent even further out. The gash in the floor crossed nearly from wall-to-wall.

That alone would have been eerie enough, but sitting in the middle of this gap, supported by several pieces of vertical floorboards, Max saw a pine-box coffin. The top had been ripped aside, discarded near the only window in the room. Max approached and saw the remains of a man long since dead — all bone and tattered clothing. The tricorn hat, brittle belt, and long-barreled musket tucked at his side suggested somebody from the late-18th or early-19th century.

"Well, well. Look at that," Drummond muttered as he flew over the coffin. "This is far better than a few trinkets on display in a museum."

Sandra stepped around the coffin. "You dug up an old body. Great. What is it you want with us?"

"For starters," Leon said, "we want to know who this is. But more importantly, we did not dig him up. When I purchased this house, it had been untouched. Two days later, I entered to find this."

"Okay. You've got a few grave robbers roaming about. Again, what is it to do with us?"

Max's shoulders slumped. "Not grave robbers, hon." He pointed to the floorboards. "If somebody had come in here and ripped this flooring open, there would be ax marks."

"He's right," Drummond said, "and the wood they chopped would have been thrown aside. This has been exploded from below or pulled up by something powerful."

"Yes," Leon said. "No ax marks. No sign of breaking and entering. Nothing to suggest grave robbers. Besides which, Mother Hope took one step in here and she knew. Something powerful, something with magical strength, brought that coffin up."

Drummond crossed his arms. "Hey, that's what I said."

"Fine," Sandra said. "You're all geniuses for noticing the lack of ax marks. That doesn't explain what you want from us, aside from identifying the remains. What is it you want us to do here?"

"Do? Nothing. You are researchers. We want you to research. Find out who the man is and why somebody would have wanted to rip him from the ground. The rest is Magi business and none of your concern."

Max could hear Sandra's blood heating up. She snapped out a finger at Leon. "If you think we're going to just run over here every time you call and solve your little mysteries without any idea of what or how that information is going to be used —"

"You forget quickly," Leon said, not even bothering to turn his face from her accusing finger. "Your husband has been cursed by Mother Hope. You'll do whatever we ask or she'll send him to the ghost world while keeping his body in a coma."

Max involuntarily reached up to his chest. The mark of Mother Hope's curse seemed to vibrate under his skin. Unless that was his raging heartbeat.

Brushing off his concerns, he looked closer at the skeleton. Dust and cobwebs clung to its broken smile. Several teeth had fallen from the skull but could be seen in the coffin near the left clavicle. In fact, other than the missing teeth, the skeleton looked remarkably preserved — except for two matters. First, the right femur was missing. Second, a dustless patch marked the skeleton's chest yet had been covered by its dusty hands.

Max said, "This man held something. From the shape, I'd say it was a book."

"Oh, yes," Leon said. "I almost forgot about that. It's a journal, we think. Haven't had much time to look at it, yet."

"I doubt that."

"Please. Max, Sandra, I have no reason to be against you. In fact, Mother Hope instructed me to help you as much as possible. She assigned me because of my experience working at the Z Smith Reynolds Library, that's all. I have to admit that doing research outside of the library walls is a bit daunting to me. So, I apologize that I removed the journal and forgot to mention it."

Before Sandra could stir up her anger again, Max said, "I certainly understand. We're all playing catch-up with the new changes."

"Exactly."

"But we're here now, and I'd like to see that journal."

"I understand entirely. It's at our Winston-Salem downtown office. I'll see that you get the address, and I'll make sure the journal is waiting for you to pick it up."

Max stared hard at Leon. His cellphone rang, but he refused to look away. This first case with the Magi would set precedents for the future, and Max wanted to make sure Leon, Mother Hope, and the entire organization knew that he and his partners would not be pushed around.

A few seconds later, Sandra's cellphone rang. She answered it but Max kept his focus on Leon. Taking the journal could not have been an accident, and it was more than a simple display of power. There was something else at work here. Drummond's earlier uneasiness echoed in Max's mind.

"Um, hon?" Sandra said. "We've got to go."

Max finally looked away. His wife's face looked pale. "What's wrong? Is PB okay?"

"He's fine." She glanced at the cellphone. "That was your mother."

A cold stone formed in his chest. "Is she ... is she ..."

"No, she's fine. She's alive. But she's here."

The stone dropped into his stomach. "Excuse me?"

"She called from PTI airport in Greensboro. We have to go pick her up right now."

"Oh, hell."

Chapter 2

MAX SET A PAPER GROCERY BAG on his kitchen counter as Sandra and his mother entered the house. He pulled out all the ingredients necessary to make chicken parmigiana and put them on the counter with a loud thump. Less than two hours since they had picked up his mother, and already he wanted to scream. She had complained that she was hungry, that they didn't serve her anything on the flight from Detroit or on the connection from Charlotte, and that she would be happy if they could simply stop someplace quick and get a bite. Max suggested some Lexington BBQ, but she didn't want anything foreign.

"It's not foreign, Mom. It's just a bit of local culture. Like eating a cheesesteak in Philly."

"I don't like cheesesteaks."

"Then how about Wendy's or KFC or something like that?"

"Fast food? That stuff is disgusting. I'm sure I can put something together when we get to your house."

So Max stopped at the grocery store on their way home. Sandra offered to make a nice meal for everybody, but Max's mother said, "I wouldn't want to bother you with such a trifle. I'll take care of it."

Luckily, Sandra took her aggression out on the arm rest, digging her nails in deep while forcing a smile. Drummond had the sense to be far away from any of this, so Max was on his own.

Before he could put water in a pot to boil, his mother grabbed an apron and started working on dinner. Sandra glowered at Max as she walked by. "I'll get the room ready for you, Mrs. Porter." From the first day these women had met, Max's mother insisted on being spoken to formally.

"No need to bother for me," Mrs. Porter said. "I can sleep down here on the couch."

"We have a guest room. I'll make the bed up right now."

"Oh, well then, thank you, dear. I didn't want to assume you had been thoughtful enough to provide a room for guests."

Sandra forced a grin before leaving. Once Max heard Sandra stomp up the stairs, he turned to his mother. "Why are you provoking her?"

"Maxwell, what are you talking about?"

"What's going on? Why did you suddenly show up unannounced?"

Chopping an onion, each cut accentuating her remarks, she said, "I think I've waited long enough to be invited, but since that clearly wasn't going to happen, I took matters into my own hands. You two think you can do whatever you want and ignore those who have taken care of you, but you're wrong. I know I taught you better. I can only assume that your wife is to blame."

"Don't start in on her. It's not her fault. In fact, she often suggested we have you down to visit."

"I doubt that." She tossed the onions into a hot pan, and they sizzled.

"Look, ever since we moved here, we've been terribly busy. It's been hard and we've had to work non-stop in order to survive."

Mrs. Porter gestured with a spatula in hand. "Yes, I can see how awful it's been living in this palace."

"This house? Not too long ago, we were in a trailer. That's right. It's only been a short time since we've been doing this well. You think I wanted you to see us when we barely had heat?"

"I'm sorry to hear you had to go through that, but how was I to know when you don't tell me anything? I could have helped you out."

Even as she tried to stir the onions, Max hugged her. It felt better than strangling her. Besides, he knew she meant it when she said she would have helped. Standing only five feet even, he had no trouble kissing the top of her head. "Thank you for the thought. But you taught me to stand on my own, and that's what I'm trying to do."

Mrs. Porter tilted her head up and gave him a motherly peck on the cheek. "You're a good boy. Even if you don't think about your ol' mother often enough."

"I'll try to be better. But you try to be nicer to Sandra."

Turning back to her cooking, Mrs. Porter said, "Do you remember Mrs. Kopinski? The lady two houses down who used to make cookies for you and your friends."

"Sure, I remember."

"Well, the other day —"

As Mrs. Porter prattled along a tale of misplaced mail, burnt cookies, and a stray cat, Max's mind wandered back to the skeleton in the empty house. The missing bone, the missing journal, and the strange manner in which the coffin had burst through the floor — all of it reeked of trouble. But more than any of that, he wondered what Mother Hope truly sought. Could she really want him simply to research this oddity? Of course, not. Max had been down this road enough times now to know better.

The doorbell had to ring three times before he looked up. Mrs. Porter had a wooden spoon in one hand and the other posed on her hip. "Have you heard anything I've said?"

Sandra hurried down the stairs to answer the door. From the hall, she called out, "It's J."

"Who's Jay?" Mrs. Porter asked as Max jumped to his feet.

Sandra and J entered the kitchen. "One of our employees, and a cutie-pie, too," she said. J entered like a shy toddler hiding behind his Mommy instead of a shy teenager embarrassed by his employer. The second-half of the Sandwich Boys, J had been homeless like his counterpart. As a black teen without parents or stability, he lived a life destined for jail or death. But he was smart and ambitious. He saw a way out and wasted no time jumping on board. After several cases with PB and J, Max had no clue how he ever got on without them.

Mrs. Porter gave J a once-over look and then nodded. "You want to help me cook dinner?"

To Max and Sandra's shock, J pushed them aside to get into the kitchen. As Mrs. Porter tied an apron around him, he glanced back. "PB's doing much better. That infection is mostly gone and he's eating good again."

"You say *well* not *good*," Mrs. Porter said.

"PB's doing *well*. Another week or so and he'll be ready to work."

Sandra said, "That's good news. I'm sure you're relieved."

"Yeah, but you don't got to worry about nothing. I'm still here, and I can do anything you need."

Max nodded. "We know. In fact, after we eat, I have an important errand for you. I need you to pick up an old journal for me. I'll give you the address and you can take my car."

Mrs. Porter raised an eyebrow. "He drives?"

"I'm pretty good at it," J said.

"You can't possibly be old enough."

He shrugged. "That only matters if I get caught."

Nobody pushed further on the topic and they all settled into casual conversation. Throughout dinner, Max and Sandra worked hard to keep all talk light and meaningless. They even successfully dodged a bullet when Mrs. Porter asked to use the serving tray she had given them as a wedding gift — an abomination to the name of serving trays (a porcelain tray with clawed feet as if it were an old bathtub) that they kept packed away in the attic. J came to the rescue, however, by asking her about a scar on her hand. That led to a story about a childhood bully she fought off in sixth grade.

The two then spent much of the evening asking each other probing questions. Mrs. Porter wanted to know how homeless life had been and what it really was like to be black in the South. J wanted to know about life in the cold, cold North and whether she thought about dying much. They were shockingly honest.

J said homelessness wasn't so bad, except in the winter. And being black was just the way his life was. He learned early on not to trust or expect much from white people, even the kind ones, and then he had no problems. "You can't get burned if you refuse to touch the fire."

For Mrs. Porter's part, she complained that the cold had gotten much worse lately. The winters were shorter but harsher, and her old bones reacted badly when the snows came. As for death, she said, "I certainly think about it more now than ever before. But you know what? I've lived a long life, and I'm not done yet. The way I think about it is that I can't control it one way or the other. So, until my number is called up, I'm going to keep living as much as I can."

J smiled. "You should work on a case with us. That'll make you feel like you're living."

Sandra choked on her food. Max wanted to leap across the table and gag the boy. Instead, he said, "It's been a long day. Let's clean up, and J, I still need you to get that journal."

Clicking her fork on her plate, Mrs. Porter said, "You are not going to let this sweet boy run through the city just to get a book. That's cruel."

"There's nothing cruel about it, and it's his job. He gets paid to help me out. Besides, he knows the streets better than any of us. And it's not like we're living in 1970s Harlem. This is Winston-Salem."

J patted Mrs. Porter's arm. "I'll be fine. It's no big deal."

"You should at least spend the night here when you get back. It'll be too late for you to go tramping around town by that point."

Sandra stood and gathered the plates a bit too harshly. "Fine. I'll make the couch up for tonight. Now, if you're done deciding how to use my house, I've got dishes to take care of."

All grew still as Sandra left the dining room. J's eyes widened in the silence. He looked to Max for assurance. With a motion of his head, Max sent J off to get the journal, and J didn't hesitate. Max's mother sat stiff as she dabbed a napkin at her mouth.

"I've apparently overstepped my bounds," she said. "I only wanted to make sure the young man was well-cared for."

"He'll be fine," Max said. "And Sandra will be fine, too."

"She doesn't like me."

"You don't like her, either."

"I wouldn't be rude to her like that."

Launching into a detailed list of all the times she had been rude to Sandra would have taken up the rest of the evening. Max held back. With a controlled, faux-calm, he said, "Since we didn't know you were coming, we weren't prepared. We've also been hired on for a new case, and that means I've got a lot of work to do tonight."

"Oh, well, I wouldn't want to be a burden. I'll stay out of your way. Don't worry. It's good that you're working. You work too hard, but I'm happy that you keep busy. I'm sure we can spend time together tomorrow."

As Mrs. Porter left for the guest room, Max heard the faucet running in the kitchen and the clatter of dishes flung into the dishwasher. He thought it best to stay out of range, but he had to pass by the kitchen in order to reach his study. No sense in poking an angry lioness. He would wait.

Several minutes later, the dishwasher rumbled on and Sandra entered the dining room. With her arms crossed and her hip popped to the side, she said, "Are you going to keep hiding out here or are we going into the study to discuss the case?"

With a bashful grin, Max said, "The case sounds like the best thing to discuss right now."

"You know it."

Settling behind his desk in his study, Max took a breath and tried to relax his muscles. Though most certainly a cliché, Max saw his study as a private sanctuary. Surrounded by books, a few sculptures, thick carpeting, and dark wood walls, Max's study remained the best part of the house in his eyes — even with his wife sitting opposite him with a heavy glower.

"How long is she staying?" Sandra asked.

"I thought we were going to talk about the case."

"The longer she stays, the more difficult our job will be. So, how long?"

Max shrugged. "I'll ask her tomorrow."

With two fingers, Sandra rubbed the center of her forehead. "I know you haven't seen her in a long time, and I know she's your mother, but I can't take too much of her. She hates me, and she's not shy about it."

"I know. I wish it wasn't so."

"Just ... please keep her out of my hair."

"You got it."

"Thanks, hon. So, this case — what do we know?"

Max leaned back in his chair. "We really haven't had time yet. Once J gets back, I'll dig into that journal, but otherwise, you know more than I do."

"Me?"

"No way did that coffin burst out of the floor naturally. That much seems clear. Something magic caused it. And if Mother Hope is calling us on the job, then it's definitely a major magic problem."

"You are the best around here at research. You don't think she could simply want you to —"

"No," Max said. His hand absently traced the circular mark on his chest — the curse Mother Hope had put upon him. "She wouldn't bother with us for minor research. Something serious is going on."

Sandra lifted her head. "I wish you weren't right, but we both know you are."

"I'll savor the rarity." He forced a chuckle. "Go get some rest. I'll wait up for J."

Chapter 3

HOURS LATER, under a blanket of quiet in the house, Max returned to his office with the newly acquired journal. J had no trouble getting it, and when he arrived at the house, Max's mother took over his care.

She insisted on fixing him a turkey sandwich and sat with him in the kitchen as he downed the meal. Then she snapped at him because he wanted to go to bed without brushing his teeth. A lecture about hygiene, including dental, ensued with the end result that J quickly showered and brushed his teeth before calling it a night on the couch.

By the time things were quiet again and Max could fall back into his office chair, the house had closed up shop. Mrs. Porter had tucked J in and promised him a pancake breakfast in the morning. Sandra bid all a goodnight before she retired to the master bedroom, not fast enough to avoid a reproach for failing to have stocked blueberries for the pancakes, but fast enough for all to let the walls in the house protect them from each other for a few sleepy hours.

Max, however, did not sleep. He read the journal — cover to cover. It belonged to a young man named Archibald Henderson. It wasn't long and the majority of entries involved the maintenance of a farm, but near the end, he chewed upon some choice nibbles.

March 7, 1769

I've been absent from writing my thoughts upon this book for too long. It is the irony of the times that I have so much to contribute here yet not enough hours to put it down. I will try, however, to bring about some understanding of what we in the back country face and have faced. Our dispute with the Royal government stretches back quite far. In point of fact, I recall clearly my father telling me about his participation in the Enfield Riot of 1758. I was but ten years of age, sitting on the floor of our tiny home. Father sat at the table while my two sisters and brother, all younger as I am the eldest, lined along the edge of our parents bed in the corner. Mother stood by the fire, cooking venison stew from the doe we had caught that morning. Such a warm memory of my family that it was not until this past year that I began to understand the importance of the tale he told us that night.

Archibald went on to relate in detail how his father and the other farmers tried to cut a living out of the difficult terrain of the back country — the interior of North Carolina, barely connected with rudimentary roads and mostly inaccessible to sea and river vessels. They were hearty folk who did not balk at the backbreaking work required of them. But they also wanted a sense of fairness in their lives.

The inequity that caused the trouble surrounded the very land they lived on. Through an odd bit of heredity, Lord Granville had fallen into owning a huge swath of North Carolina that cut a line halfway across the state. Everything north of the line (and reaching into modern day Virginia) belonged to him.

Granville had little interest in owning this land but great interest in selling it for a large profit. The Crown had laws concerning how land in the New World would be cut up and sold, but even then, the Crown had difficulty controlling matters so far from home. Few of the governors paid attention to the Crown's fee schedule, and instead, adopted convoluted and arbitrary rules for acquiring land. This had the desired effect of keeping the rabble from gaining too much land.

"And at that time," Max muttered to the journal, "land ownership equaled voting rights."

All Father wanted back then was a voice. It is still all we desire. Back then, Father and almost five hundred men walked into the lower house of the legislature with complaints against Francis Corbin and Joshua Bodley.

Five hundred men.

Corbin and Bodley had been among the worst offenders of abusing the land laws. They had milked the back-country folk for every bit of money they could squeeze out.

"But five hundred men in the 1750s was enough to scare the local government bad."

Between Archibald's journal and a few quick Google searches, Max discovered that Corbin and Bodley fled. They made it as far as Edgecombe County before getting caught. Lucky for them, these "backwards" farmers were not bloodthirsty. They simply wanted a fair deal on the land and a voice in the government. They thought they had won that day. But corruption would never be defeated so easily.

"Max, you awake?" Drummond called out before sliding through the far wall.

Rubbing his eyes, Max said, "Yeah, come on in. You find anything?"

"Don't have much to go on. No name, no identifying bits. Basically, we got a dead guy from Revolutionary times. You know how many ghosts in the Other fit the description?"

"Actually, no."

"A lot. Hundreds."

Setting the journal on the table, Max tapped the top of it. "Well, we got a name now. Archibald Henderson."

"Anything else? You know yet why he's trying to break out of his coffin?"

"We don't even know if that's what happened. It's clear that his family came from the back country and they were involved in some of the precursors to the American Revolution. That's all I got so far."

Drummond pursed his lips. "Any idea what's really going on here? I mean with Mother Hope and the Magi."

"Haven't a clue. But I'm glad to see that you're thinking it, too. I can't believe this is just some simple research."

"Is there such a thing when it comes to our cases?"

"Exactly." Max warmed at the reassurance — even if it

meant that something darker hung over them all. "I guess we've got to keep digging. I'll get back to the journal. You—"

"I know. Back to the Other. See if I can find Archibald Henderson."

"Good luck. We'll meet up at the office in the morning."

Drummond brought his collar tighter around his neck. "Will your mother be coming?"

"Charming as ever. No, I'll try to keep her clear."

"Thanks. I don't mean to be rude to you, but I can only take small doses of people like that."

Max tried not to be offended. He knew his mother rubbed many the wrong way. But she was his mother. And she could be kind, too.

"Good night, Drummond."

"Night, Max."

Max sat alone in his office for a little. Cool air followed the whoosh of the central air kicking on. He brushed his fingers over the journal. Almost two hundred and fifty years old and here it sat on his desk, under his fingers, divulging its secrets only to him. It seemed as if there should be some ceremony before he read it again, but he would have to settle for standing up, stretching his arms over his head, and grabbing a drink of water from the kitchen.

Heading back to his study, he heard murmured voices from the living room. He stopped and listened closer. Inching down the hall, Max maneuvered near enough to see his mother tucking J into the makeshift bed on the couch.

She beamed at the teen. "You listen to me. Your life is important. Don't go wasting it on stupid risks. Okay? And I'm not talking about running around at night. I've lived a long life. I know a thing or two, and I see that you can handle yourself well. But that kind of surety brings along with it arrogance, and arrogance can get you hurt."

"Don't worry about me," J said, with his cocky *I'm the man* voice. "I'm always a step ahead."

Max cringed, bracing himself for the tirade his mother would now unleash. But she laughed — a short, quiet sound unlike anything he had ever heard from her.

"You get some sleep," she said. "Can I get you anything before I go?"

J actually snuggled further into the couch. "Thanks. You're a sweet lady."

"I'm glad somebody here thinks so."

Popping up on his elbow, J frowned. "Why is that? I mean, why are you and Sandra so mad at each other?"

"I'm not mad at Sandra. Really, I'm not. But I think Max could have done better. He could have found a woman who made him happy. That's all parents ever really want for their children. I don't care if Max is rich or poor — as long as he's happy."

"You don't think he's happy with Sandra?"

"Whenever we talk on the phone, I can hear the tension in his voice. Ever since they got married, they've struggled, and he never sounds content, let alone happy. Look at this place. It's gorgeous. But do they enjoy it? They look as stressed as ever. Do they cling to each other? Help each other through? I don't know for sure, but it doesn't seem so. Never has." She re-tucked J's blanket. "Max is my boy. You understand? My child. It hurts me to see him this way, and it angers me to see the source of that being the person who should be loving him, not hurting him."

"Hey, at least they're together. My folks split up when I was a baby. Then they both split town. I ain't ever had anybody care enough even to be mad at me."

"Don't say *ain't*."

J glanced around the room. "Fact is, Max and Sandra and my pal, PB — they're the closest thing I got to family. So, even if they are a bit messed up, they're better than nothing."

Mrs. Porter leaned over and kissed J's forehead. "If they're your family, then that makes me your family, too. I guess I'm your new grandma."

He smiled. "Cool."

Before she could leave J's side, Max hurried back to his study. He banged into his chair with a clumsy escape like an amateur. He stared at the journal on his desk, even reached out to open it and get back to work, but he pulled his hand away.

In all his years, she had never spoken to him like that. Never shown him such affection, such warmth, such understanding. Or had she? Did he simply ignore those memories because they didn't fit a narrative he had constructed about his relationship with her?

With a jolt, Max straightened in his chair. "Oh, man. Am I jealous?"

Chapter 4

MAX AND SANDRA USUALLY spent their mornings drinking coffee, eating some toast or bagels, and reading the news on their phones. They might talk a little, but only if they had both slept soundly the night before. When the sun rose that following morning, however, the Porter house rattled with activity.

Mrs. Porter clattered pans and plates as she nailed off pancakes, toast, and bacon with the expert efficiency of a pro — which Max fully admitted, she was. Coffee brewed while J thumped about the breakfast table, placing plates and silverware with plenty of noise and cheer. Mrs. Porter hummed a tune that Max recognized long before he entered the kitchen — a meandering melody of her own creation that accompanied her whenever she worked around the house.

"Good morning," Max said. Sandra had yet to reach the talking stage of waking up. She followed him to the table.

J handed them each a paper napkin. "We made you breakfast."

"Thanks. We could both use some coffee to start."

Mrs. Porter carried over a hot pan of eggs. "Sit down, J. Max can get the coffee. You're a growing boy. You need to eat."

J looked at Max and rolled his eyes, but he could not hide his delight in being treated his age. *A bit less than his age,* Max thought.

Near the end of the morning meal, Max downed the last of his coffee and said, "Mom, I'm sorry but you'll be on your own today. I didn't know you were coming, so we've got work that has to be done."

"That's fine."

"I'm real sorry. I know you were expecting —"

"I said it was fine. No need to worry about me. I can entertain myself. I do it all the time back home. Besides, as long as you don't need this young man, I think we will go to the zoo together."

"The zoo?" Max said.

"The zoo!" J said.

Mrs. Porter brushed toast crumbs into her napkin. "Why not? It's not that far. You don't mind letting us borrow a car, do you?"

"Sure. Go ahead," Max said, though a sharp pain formed in his chest.

Sandra, on the other hand, let out an audible sigh. "I need a shower," she managed. As she left the kitchen, she added, "Thanks for breakfast."

An hour later, Max and Sandra parked on Liberty Street and walked to their downtown office. On the short drive, he brought Sandra up to speed on the case, but before they entered the building, he halted. "Do you mind taking care of the office work this morning? I want to go to the library and check out a few things."

Though Sandra said nothing, Max knew that she understood. He would do the research, but he also needed some space. No other place gave him sanctuary like the library — in particular, the Z. Smith Reynolds Library at Wake Forest University.

The library consisted of two old academic buildings that had been reformed into one. The former alley between them had been walled in and topped with tempered glass that let sunlight fill the area. What would have been outside walls now boasted balconies that looked over this garden-like space, and instead of plants growing, young minds blossomed as they studied at the tables spread out below.

The Zen quality of any library compounded in this particular place, and Max needed that now. He needed to focus on the case, but his mind refused to quiet. He kept thinking about his mother and J and their budding relationship. Why should she suddenly be doting on this young man? Did she truly have a connection with J or was this some passive-aggressive way to strike at Max? She wanted to be a grandmother. Could this situation be nothing grander than a surrogate?

Whatever the case, he could not deny how much it bothered him. While part of him wanted to mull over the whole thing, the rest of him knew he had to take advantage of the limited time he had been given. Because no matter what else, Mother Hope had brought this case to them, and that still bothered him more than anything his mother could do.

Setting up at one of the library's computer stations, Max began with a search for Archibald Henderson. The first hit surprised him. Brigadier General Archibald Henderson held the distinction of being the longest-serving Commandant of the Marine Corps — from 1820 to 1859. Unfortunately, he was born in January 1783 — well past the Revolution. Not the man they sought.

After numerous other attempts to find Henderson, Max had to accept the logical result — Archibald Henderson was not a man who made it into the history books. All they had was the man's journal. A great primary resource, but limited by the man's infrequent entries.

"Wait," Max said. "The entries."

Henderson had written about his father's involvement in the Enfield Riot. Perhaps the father could be found. Max searched the Enfield Riot and dug into his work.

Over the next few hours, he went through various accounts and reports. Unfortunately, with around five hundred farmers participating, Max could not find the name Henderson. Indeed, most of the names involved had been erased from history, leaving only the major players.

Max did stumble upon a reference to the Sugar Creek War which occurred six years after the Enfield Riot. Experience taught him to follow this kind of lead. What emerged from his research built a large picture of the situation.

Governor Tryon had become the leading authority in North Carolina, but he did little to tamp down the corruption that had caused dissent among the back country folk. Though called a "war," the various protests that comprised these events were often less violent and more about public shaming and humiliation. Even the Enfield Riot was less a riot in the modern sense and more like an intense gathering of a mob. Not to be discounted, but hardly a full-scale riot.

Several names kept appearing in Max's research, and he jotted down each one that he found in numerous texts. Edmund Fanning and William Tryon on the English side of things and Herman Husband on the back country side. Husband started out merely as a facilitator for those trying to get land from the old Granville Parcels and ended up being a major player in the group that would be called the Regulators.

He had heard of the Regulators before — a semi-organized group considered to be precursors to the Revolutionary forces. He also knew that researching them would take most of the afternoon. Max's stomach grumbled, and he gave it a gentle pat. He decided to listen to his body and grab some food before jumping back in. As he put his things together, he checked out three books — might as well start while he ate.

From the library, Max cut across the grounds, went by the biology building, through a student parking lot, and onto a walking path through the surrounding woods. This short, well-maintained path led to the Reynolda House shops which included a handful of places to eat. The Village Tavern could be pricey and seating was limited, but Max wanted to treat himself — or, at least, ease his worries with the sensory pleasures of a good steak.

Nicking a table in the back corner, he ordered a Delmonico and opened one of the three books he had lugged along. Before he could read a word, however, a young man paused long enough to grab Max's attention. The man had his head cocked to the side as he read the spines of Max's books.

"You interested in the Regulators?" the man asked.

Max smiled. "A bit of a hobby."

The man had a distinctive, dark look. His cheeks sunk in a little, and his eyes popped out a little. Dark, shaggy hair softened an angular nose while a lean but strong body gave him an authoritative presence. He reminded Max of the way some movie stars could be seen as intensely attractive despite having unattractive features. Something about the combination of the parts mesmerized the audiences. On some level, this man's charm had worked on Max because as he sat at the table uninvited, Max cleared a book out of the way.

"My name is Edward," the man said, offering his hand. He spoke with a rich North Carolinian accent that drew a person in to whatever he said.

Max shook the hand and gestured to the books. "You have an interest in this?"

"Very much so. I'm a history grad student. I love the stuff. But my favorite period is the American Revolution. My dissertation will be on something to do with that time. Once I can lock down what part to focus on."

"What about the Regulators? You know much about them?" Might as well mine the kid for information. A researcher always had to take advantage of the sources available.

Before he answered, Edward's eye twitched. Nothing more than a slight spasm, yet it changed the shape of the man's face. Only for a fraction of a second, but Max shivered. Then, Edward's face returned to a smile.

"I know a lot about them. They were the kicking off point of the Revolution. Not as violent as many think, though. I mean, they spent years just complaining, marching on government steps, signing petitions, and writing op-eds, that kind of thing."

"Yeah. I noticed there was a long gap between the Enfield Riot and the Sugar Creek War."

"That's right," Edward said, leaning forward with his elbows on the table. "Even after it all boiled over, even after the big battle at Alamance, many of the Regulators fought for the British during the War. Hard to call those ones traitors since the United States didn't exist yet, but still, as far as I see it, they were traitors."

"They were farmers, not soldiers."

"True. I mean they really just wanted a fair shake at getting land, not being overtaxed, and having a real voice in the government." Edward lowered his head, and the dark restaurant brought out that unsettling flicker on his face. "But what gets me mad at them is that the deeper cause underlying everything was the divide between the rich and the poor. It was a big gap, with no such thing as a middle class, and the rich kept rigging the system to make it worse. Now, that's nothing shockingly new, but even after the Regulators had a few small successes, even after they had major losses, when it all was over, what did they do? They got paid off and joined up with their enemy. Never made much sense to me."

Forcing levity into his tone, Max said, "It's like you said — nothing really new there. People have always been looking out for themselves first."

"Not me." Edward spoke with a fierce strength, low and dark, that made every word drip with threat. "I think we have a duty to our country, our people. I'm not like Archibald Henderson."

Max's head snapped up as his pulse quickened. The smell of cooking beef reminded him that he had not been served his food. He wasn't hungry anymore, but why hadn't the waitress interrupted them yet? His eyes searched for her, but she had managed to disappear. Hearing the tremble in his voice, he asked, "Who are you?"

Edward grinned at him, a toothy, wolfish grin. "I'm the one telling you quite clearly that you are on the wrong side of this."

"Wrong side of what? All I'm doing is reading some history books."

"Not all history books know the truth."

"What's this about? What do you want?"

"You have a choice, Mr. Porter. You and your wife can turn away from this, forget about Henderson, forget about the Regulators, and go on with your little research firm. Or you can keep stoking the flames that you don't even realize surround you. Do that and the fire will burn hot."

Max's jaw jutted out as he brought his face close to Edward.

"Since you obviously know who I am, I have to wonder what kind of idiot you are."

Edward hesitated. "Watch yourself."

"There's no shame in being mentally disadvantaged. Clearly, you aren't too bright. How else to explain your behavior?"

"I came here as a courtesy to warn you —"

"You came to threaten me. But my wife and I have taken down the Hull family, the most powerful wielders of magic in the area. You think you can intimidate me?"

Whatever advantage Max had gained by his bluster, it vanished in a blink. Edward pulled back, but the movement carried with it a dollop of condescension, and when he spoke, he layered on a thick amount of pity. "The Hulls boasted a lot but brought about little results. That you and your wife defeated them is not as impressive a feat as you think. They were bound to fail. You were simply the catalyst."

"If you're really a history student, you must major in revisionism."

A smirk crossed Edward's mouth. "Witchcraft existed long before the Hulls, and it will continue on long after. The Magi are no better, and Mother Hope is a newborn fawn when compared to the infinite lifespan of magic."

Max suppressed the urge to shiver. Though he still didn't know the connection between Archibald's skeleton and magic — Edward's comments were about as close to a confirmation as Max would ever get. Whatever was at the heart of all this, it had to do with magic.

Edward gracefully stood. "That's it, Mr. Porter. Walk away and you'll be unharmed. Keep moving in on this, and you and Sandra will suffer for it."

Max considered a sarcastic remark, but Edward turned on his heel and strolled out of the restaurant. Max took a few breaths and went through the entire exchange in his head — he needed to remember as many details while they were still fresh. Less than a minute later, the waitress returned with his steak as if nothing had happened.

He cut the meat and placed a juicy piece into his mouth. He

gave the conversation another whirl in his head. Eating in silence, he reached the point where he could no longer tell if he remembered correctly or had started to put in details that did not exist.

After his meal, he hurried back to the office. From the outside, the building looked like a relic from Drummond's days — tall windows, nine foot ceilings, and detailed moldings around every doorway and lining the floor and ceiling. The inside, however, boasted all the amenities a modern office could provide — thick carpets, computers, central air, and enough space for both Max and Sandra's large desks. They had a bookcase built into the wall for Drummond — it had been his ghostly home for decades in their former office.

"Any luck?" Sandra said, keeping her focus on her computer screen.

Placing a stack of books on his desk, Max said, "Well, we knew this would happen, but part of me was still taken off guard. This case has become far more serious."

Drummond poked his head from the bookcase. "Let me guess. You got threatened."

"How did you know that?"

"Same thing happened to me in the Other."

"What?" Sandra said. "What happened? To both of you."

Max related his story in as much detail as he could recall. His repetition over lunch helped him keep it straight, and by the end, he felt confident that he had not missed anything key. Looking over at Drummond, he said, "What about you?"

"No luck on finding Archibald Henderson. Not yet, at least. But like you, my searching around got me some unwanted attention. Couple of mugs followed me most of the morning. I didn't recognize them, but I wouldn't be surprised at all if I had busted them back in my police force days — several times. Some jailbirds never want to leave."

"And they threatened you?" Sandra asked.

"Jumped me in a less populated section of the Other. One held my arms back while the other gave me a few lefts and a right. Stuck mostly to my gut. Man, I haven't been punched that hard since I was living. Other types of pain, yeah plenty of that. But a solid gut punch? If it hadn't hurt so bad, I would've been thanking them for the memory."

"Did they say anything?"

"You can't really threaten all that well unless you make a threat. They told me to stop looking for Henderson. Said if I was really smart, I'd drop you two and get on with moving on."

Max tapped a pen against his chin. "Lucky for us, you're not that smart."

"Hey!"

"I meant you're not going to listen to them."

"That better be all you meant."

Sandra raised her voice above the bickering. "We've got two ghost thugs and a jerk named Edward. No last name. That's not much to go on."

"We also got the journal and the name Archibald Henderson," Drummond said. "And don't worry about those guys who assaulted me. After they left me, I followed them for a bit. Never did find who they worked for, but I did corner one and gave him a one-two that clocked him to the ground. Based on the look in his eyes, I don't think I'll be hearing from them anytime soon."

"Do we have more than enough to suggest it's all connected?" Before Max could protest that technically they had little proof beyond a few words that Edward had said, Sandra put out her hand to stop him. "We don't have to prove it. We know there's a connection because otherwise, we're looking at a mother-lode of coincidences."

"You got that right, doll."

"Which means that we're once more, back in the realm of magic and ghosts. Unless Edward has developed a machine that allows him to chat with ghost thugs and hire them out to rough up a ghost detective."

Drummond flew over to Max. "We know it started with ripping up that coffin. But we don't know the reason behind it or what it's going to lead to or even how it was done. Just asking a few questions and starting the preliminary research got us both threatened. Now, I'm not about to insult either of you and suggest that you're going to heed those warnings. In fact, I'd say you know what we need to do."

Max nodded. "Research the hell out of this."

Chapter 5

MAX CHECKED THE WALL CLOCK — 1:25 pm. His mother and J would be at the zoo for most of the day, and she would undoubtedly make him dinner. Probably even take him out for ice cream — though J preferred frozen yogurt, Max didn't see him putting up a fuss.

"We've got the rest of the day to get as much info as we can." He snapped his fingers and pointed at Drummond. "You've got to find Henderson."

Drummond thrust his hands in his pockets. "Not sure what more I can do. I got my contacts working on it. But if Edward sent those goons after me, then they certainly are tracking down anybody else poking into Henderson. My contacts are good but they're also in it for themselves. They won't risk getting beaten to a pulp just to help us out."

"All the more reason for you to head back to the Other. Your contacts might be afraid of a fight, but you're not."

Drummond grinned. "Will you look at that? The kid's learning. Appealing to my masculinity like a pro."

"Did it work?"

"Yeah, I'll go. Just once, I'd like for you guys to be stuck in there while I'm back here."

Sandra scoffed. "Do you understand that Max'll have his nose buried in books while you're out being a detective?"

"Fair point. I'll stick to what I know."

"If you can't find Henderson," she went on, "you ought to look for any ghost that was a Regulator. Maybe somebody else can shed light on this case for us."

"Good thinking. I've said it before, but Max is a lucky man to have you in his life. You're a helluva smart gal."

With a wink and a tip of his hat, Drummond disappeared.

Max paused to look upon his wife. Drummond was right, of course. He was lucky, and she was smart. Right now, he needed that brain of hers.

"Hon, you still have your old real estate contacts?"

"Of course." She brought up a file on her computer. "Once I started working with you, I made sure to keep those contacts alive. You never know when you'll need one. I'm guessing you want me to look into the history of the house we found Henderson in."

"Exactly. I'll get cracking on these books, see what I can learn about the whole Regulator movement, and if I'm lucky, find some reference to Henderson."

"What about my other contacts? I'm not familiar with the magic used here, but I'm a novice at the whole witch thing. I could call up a few people, see what they say."

Max tried to hide his expression. Sandra's interest in witchcraft had grown stronger ever since becoming friends with Maria Cortez-Kane, a hobby witch of sorts. Even after the showdown that destroyed the Hulls, even after seeing what became of their once-powerful witch, Dr. Connor, even after Maria shut the doors and refused Sandra's calls — after all of it, Sandra still wanted to become a witch. Though it would be a useful skill set to have in the firm, Max tried to temper his wife's enthusiasm on the subject. Witchcraft could consume a person, then spit out a being that looked the same but whose heart had been carved out and left empty.

"Let's hold off on the witches until we have a better idea of what we're dealing with," he said, forcing his tone to stay low and calm.

Sandra drew to attention and offered a mock salute. "Aye-aye, Cap'n." Then she leaned forward and kissed him gently. "I can see the worry on your face. This Edward guy really got you, huh?"

"No. Maybe. I don't like people threatening to harm you. I know we've been through a lot of crazy in the last few years, I know you're tough and capable, but there's a primitive side of me that wants to protect you."

She kissed him again. "You're a sweet man, Maxwell Porter."

"Oh, don't call me that. Only my mother calls me Maxwell."

"I'm well aware of that." She laughed. "Now, come on. You've had your moment of doubt. Can we move on to the point where you buckle down and figure this all out?"

Chuckling, Max said, "Am I that predictable?"

"Hon, when it comes to solving this kind of thing, I'm always going to bet on you — because, yes, you're predictably good at this."

With that, they got to work.

A few hours in and Max had developed a clearer picture of the Regulator movement and how it related to the American Revolution. It all came down to a long, slow simmer of anger that developed over the course of decades. People can handle a bit of corruption in their government. In fact, most people expect it. But when that corruption becomes flagrant and when the divide between rich and poor becomes outrageous, then that slow simmer starts to boil. That was what happened in North Carolina.

"It all came down to a sense of entitlement," Max said to his books.

The corrupt land system only received patches that were designed to look like the government had fixed the issues upsetting the back country people, but in reality, the changes only made things worse. It manifested in little things at times such as the road crews. The law stated that anybody who lived near a road, whether free or slave, had to work on a road crew to maintain that section. However, there were loopholes that made it easy for the rich to avoid the work. The poor noticed.

It also manifested in larger events like Tryon's Palace. Governor Tryon wanted to construct a massive residence that could double as a central government office. A White House long before the White House existed. He commissioned detailed plans and broke ground. But when the state and county money dried up, he brazenly used taxes to pay for the endeavor.

Any one of these types of things would cause the people to grumble. But added together, the people started to talk to each other, to organize, and soon the Regulator movement was born. Their simple goal rested in their name — they wanted real regulation to rein in the out-of-control government.

Max jotted down a few notes. "No government official would go along with that easily."

More injustices occurred. Several meetings took place but little progress happened. At one point, Herman Husband and other locals managed to get seen by the Grand Jury, only to find that when they showed up, the jury had been stacked with the very people the locals were upset about. Then in May 1768, Governor Tryon had Husband arrested.

"Not a smart move."

As Max expected, arresting Husband only galvanized the locals against Tryon. Around one thousand men surrounded the town of Hillsborough and demanded his release. Tryon complied but, later that year, he made sure the Hillsborough District Superior Court washed clean his tarnished record. To insure his success and to avoid any Regulator disruption, he marched in with troops as a clear threat of force.

"The amazing thing," Max said to Sandra, startling her from her own research, "in all this history is how the English had so many opportunities to avoid the Revolution. I mean look at this. Even after decades of corruption and abuse of power, the Regulators still attempted to fix things in a peaceful manner. They started running for and winning local offices, trying to change things by legal means. They even drafted yet another petition outlining their problems, but this one is a legal document, not simply a complaint, and it's intended for King George to read. And, get this — this'll show you how serious things got to be — they needed somebody to deliver the petition and they wanted an agent unconnected to Tryon that all sides could trust. So, who do the get?"

Sandra played along, smiling at his enthusiasm. "Tell me, oh genius of the historical texts."

"Benjamin Franklin. Can you believe that?"

"Actually, I can. Wasn't he constantly acting as an Ambassador of sorts?"

"I know, but this is 1768 — nearly a decade before the Revolution."

"Well, Benjamin Franklin didn't appear on the scene fully-formed. He had to get his start somewhere."

"Exactly my point. Each piece leads to the next. If the English had simply dealt fairly with the people of North Carolina instead of trying to grab as much for themselves as they could, then the Battle of Alamance would never have happened, and many consider that the first true defiant battle against the Crown. The precursor battle of the Revolution."

"Brilliant work." Sandra threw a pen at him. "Now, maybe you can turn the focus onto something about Archibald Henderson?"

"This is. Remember, his journal references some of the early actions that led to Alamance."

He went on to explain that in May 1771, the Battle of Alamance changed the situation for everybody. It began like most of the other incidents — with a large group of back country folk pulling together in protest. Had the English simply let the protest happen and peter out on its own, it would have been nothing special or unique.

But Tryon had reached his limit. Plus, he had pressures from outside: people questioning his ability to control North Carolina, people wanting to make a profit off him and frustrated by profitless inaction, political motivations, and a personal distaste for these low-class types. He marched his troops in, including eight cannons.

The cannons of the time did not have much range but they still packed a whollop. Tryon went through all the formal steps — displaying the superior force he held, sending messengers to the Regulators demanding surrender, and giving final warnings. But the Regulators, thinking they were involved in another protest that might turn a little violent but mostly would be a lot of posturing, played along.

Until Tryon opened fire.

"The Regulators never stood a chance. They were ridiculously out-gunned, and they had no serious military organization among themselves — no General to order movements, no serious fire power beyond the weapons they usually used for hunting, and no training to hold ground in the face of a terrifying force. The battle went fast, and the Regulators scattered."

Max got to his feet, speaking rapidly as he moved around the room. "Here's where it gets even more interesting. After the battle, the Regulators fall apart. Many of them pack up, go home, and that's it for their involvement in any kind of rebellion. Quite a few join up with the English in a bit of *if you can't beat 'em, join 'em* mentality. And many of the others remain upset and eventually help fight in the Revolution. But before all of that, shortly after the battle, Tryon rounds up twelve men suspected or known to be involved with the Regulators and their attempted rebellion at Alamance. Six of these men are hanged."

"You think Henderson was one of those six?"

"I thought so, at first." Max scurried to his desk to check his notes. "We know four of the men hanged — Benjamin Merrill, James Pugh, Captain Messer, and Robert Matear. But the last two are unknown. But then I checked Henderson's journal."

"Let me guess — he's got entries after the hanging."

"Yup. After Alamance, he becomes very vague whenever he writes about anything even remotely related to the Regulators. I think the whole thing scared him bad. But whatever his connection, I don't see anything that suggests witchcraft. No spooky stories about the six hanged men walking the battlefield at night or some cursed family that traces its lineage back to those men, or anything like that."

While Max reported his results, Sandra had been working on her computer. Nodding half to herself and half to Max's tale, she said, "So, we don't know much really. Unfortunately, I don't have much here, either."

"What are you looking at?"

"My real estate friend sent me a history on the house. It was built in 1927 by Mr. Jackson Gates. Changed hands a few times over the decades, nothing that stands out as strange, until it's finally bought by Mother Hope. Technically, it was bought by Raymond Watterson. I'm guessing Mother Hope uses various Magi to front for her purchases." She clicked a few times to bring up her other research. "Now, the only weird thing is that the land the house sits on traces back to around 1780 and the Moravians."

Max sat on the edge of his desk. "What's so weird about that? They founded Winston and Salem. I would expect almost all of the land here to have once belonged to them."

"The weird part isn't that they owned the land. It's that their ownership doesn't go back any further. The Moravians were in North Carolina well before 1780, and that house isn't in some remote section of the area. It was prime real estate."

"So, who owned it?"

"I'm not sure, yet."

The phone rang and Max jumped. "Hello, Porter Agency."

"It's Leon Moore." Leon sounded out of breath.

"What do you want?"

"Got another body for you to look at."

"Wasn't much of a body the first time around."

"A skeleton, then. Just get over here right away."

Grabbing a pad and pen, Max said, "Have a little patience. We'll get there. Don't worry."

"Quit being a smart-ass. I'm trying to keep this thing protected but if the police do a sweep, I'm going to have to run."

"The police? Where the heck are you?"

"The Bog Garden in Greensboro. I don't know if the police, or anybody, sweeps through the park before closing the gates, but I'm not taking any chances. Get your ass out here."

Leon hung up without waiting for a reply. Max set the phone down, considering whether to hurry out to Greensboro or do nothing and cross his fingers that Leon would get caught by the cops.

"Well?" Sandra said. "I can see on your face that something happened."

Letting Leon hang out in jail for several hours while the cops try to figure out why they found him near a centuries-old corpse would be fun, but then Max would have a tough time getting the answers he sought. And he had to admit it — doing the research and unraveling even a small chunk of this mess had excited him.

Max snatched his keys off the desk. "Grab your coat. We're going on a field trip."

Chapter 6

By the time Max and Sandra parked their car at the Friendly Shopping Center in Greensboro, the sun had set. Located off Friendly Avenue, the shopping complex filled enough acreage to build a large housing development upon. People bustled about the various restaurants and stores while a number of cars headed for the multiplex movie theater. The Bog Garden was behind a specialty soap store in the northern corner of the center, across Northline Avenue and surrounded by houses on the other sides.

Max led the way by two dumpsters and down a grassy hill. They crossed the street and walked along the metal fencing that lined the park. The gates closed at dusk, but they were designed to keep cars out, not people. Max and Sandra slipped around the posts that held the gate up and strolled along the well-groomed park.

"Over here," Leon said, stepping out from behind a group of pine trees. "Follow me."

At a quick pace, he moved along the dirt path. Soon it became a gravel path and after that wood-shavings marked the way. Finally, they climbed up to a running boardwalk. Wood slats and railings cut through the bog like rails in the forest — a man-made pathway that disturbed the natural beauty of the area while attempting to protect it at the same time.

Max halted. He heard something. Looking back over his shoulder, he squinted into the dark.

"Come on," Leon said.

"I heard —"

"Squirrels and chipmunks. This park is overrun with the vermin."

Leon pushed onward and they followed, but Max continued

to peek back now and then.

"Where exactly are we going?" Sandra asked.

"The bog opens up into a lake. The body is at the edge." Leon waved vaguely ahead. "You're lucky I got here in time. I had to chase off a young guy."

Max said, "What did he look like? Dark hair, good-looking sort?"

"I wasn't really worried about that. I figured making sure Mother Hope had something to show you two was more important. Besides, after he ran off, I had to jump under the walk to avoid the park sweep."

In the dark, Max had difficulty telling for sure, but Leon's back did look wet. Even if Leon lied about that much, Max suspected the first part to be true. Though he couldn't prove it, his gut told him that their uninvited guest had to be Edward Wallace.

He glanced back into the darkness once more. Did he see something move? Probably a branch or a small animal. Probably.

Sandra drew his attention back when she nailed a vital question. "How did you find this body, anyway? The first one makes sense. You guys bought the house and stumbled upon the body. But out here?"

Leon walked stiffer. "That's not important."

"Actually, it is," Max said. "We need every bit of the picture in order to do our job properly. I'm sure Mother Hope would want us to be fully-informed, or else we wouldn't be able to give her what she needs to know."

"Mother Hope is the one who instructed me to come here, and so I did. I did not question her nor would I ever do so. If you want answers to those questions, you'll have to ask her yourself. But I'm telling you now, she won't like it."

The boardwalk path split off east and west. They took the eastern path which ended in an octagonal viewing station like a fancy end to a dock. Leon climbed over the waist-high railing and splashed below.

Though right in the middle of a heavily populated area, the

bog remained dark. Max could hear the steady shushing of cars driving by and the occasional boom of a radio playing music too loud for the speakers to handle well. Through the trees, he could spot the flicker of light from nearby homes. Despite this, he had a sense of cold isolation.

"Come on," Leon said, adopting a harsh whisper. Perhaps he felt it, too.

Max turned on his flashlight and peered down. "You could've warned us to wear some boots or something."

Leon stood shin-deep in mud. "It's called the Bog Garden. What did you expect?"

Climbing over the railing, Sandra said, "Let's get this over with."

"Fine," Max said, rolling his shoulders. "But if we have to replace any of our clothes, I'm billing the Magi for it." He snatched a peek back into the woods — he couldn't be sure, but he thought he caught a shadow that looked distinctly human in shape. When he stepped closer, he only saw trees with odd-shaped branches.

"Max, quit stalling," Sandra snapped.

"I'm coming. Sheesh." He sat on the railing, swung his legs over, and dropped into the mud with a splash.

"Hey!" Leon shook the splattered mud from his arms.

"Sorry." Scanning the bog with his flashlight, Max said, "Where's the body?"

"Over here," Sandra said.

She stood several feet from the boardwalk. A thick growth of low plants blanketed the soggy ground and four tall bushes formed a foliage wall that blocked the body from sight. Max slogged up beside his wife and gazed behind the bushes.

A pine coffin lay half-submerged in the murky water. The surrounding mud piled up its side while other clumps dotted the area in a clear circle as if the coffin had erupted from beneath. Its top had been ripped off and tossed into the heavy bushes. The skeleton inside smiled at them.

Unlike Archibald Henderson, this skeleton had not survived intact. Many of its bones were missing, and those that remained were stained with mud and decay. Where Henderson had been buried with his hat, journal, and musket, this one looked to have been dumped aside. If not for the similar way the coffins appeared to have exploded forth, Max would have seen nothing to connect the two.

Sandra moved first. The depth of the mud varied greatly, making the simple act of walking to the coffin a chore. One step brought her leg down to the knee in mud. The next only went ankle deep. In the darkening night, it was difficult to judge where to place the next step.

"Look here," she said.

Max sighed and Sandra chuckled. They both knew he wouldn't be able to walk away — not until he examined the coffin for himself. With tentative steps, he attempted to follow the path Sandra had led while avoiding her missteps along the way. Leon remained by the boardwalk. Hopefully, he guarded the area, keeping alert to any unusual sounds or motions.

"What do you got?" Max asked when he reached her side.

She pointed her flashlight right below the skull. A small bag, probably made of deerskin, had been tied around the neck and now rested against the skeleton's clavicle. Max reached for the bag but Sandra slapped his hand. "You don't want to touch that."

"What is it?"

"A curse, I think. I've seen pictures in my books on witchcraft. Bags like that are used for all sorts of magic."

"Like a juju bag?"

"Sort of. It helps focus the spell and it can also serve as a surrogate circle. Whoever wanted to curse this man either didn't have the time or the ability to draw a curse into the coffin."

"And this is the next best thing."

"Exactly."

"Which confirms beyond a doubt that there is magic involved in this. I'll bet we'll find one of these bags in Archibald Henderson's coffin, too."

"More than likely."

Max used his flashlight to inspect the bones from top to bottom. "Look there," he said, pointing at the skeleton's legs. "Both femurs."

"I guess Leon didn't have time to steal one." Sandra leaned closer. "Oh." She cocked her head to the side. "There's something written on the right one."

"Written?"

"Symbols. A few numbers. Definitely witchcraft."

"Take it."

Sandra shot bolt upright. "What?"

"We can't study it here, and I swear we're being watched. Take the bone and we'll check it out at the office."

"There might be two curses on this man, and you want me to just take the bone. Don't you think that might cause us some problems?"

Max glanced over his shoulder — he could barely see Leon poke a stick in the mud. "Hon, Leon stole the femur from Henderson. That's not a coincidence."

"We don't know it was him."

"It was somebody. And if we're going to stay ahead of whatever game Mother Hope and Edward Wallace are playing, we need that bone. Now, you said it might be cursed. Are you not sure?"

"Don't start that. I admit I'm a novice, but that doesn't mean I'm an idiot." She glared at him, but he put on his most-innocent, puppy-dog look. "Okay. I don't know for sure if these are curses, but there is definite magic involved here, and that means we should be cautious. Very cautious."

Max nodded. "You got a suggestion?"

Sandra wrinkled her brow. "How about this — we take the bone and bury it someplace secluded. Then we make contact with a witch who would know how to read it, and if she says it's safe, we'll dig it up and bring it in."

"Sounds good."

She thrust her flashlight at him. "Hold this." Repositioning closer to the coffin, she reached out toward the bone. Her hands shook, and Max could see the glint of trepidation in her eye like wincing in expectation of a shock. The skeleton smiled upon her, its eye sockets dark voids that watched her nonetheless.

When she touched the leg bone, Max braced himself for an alarm to ring out or flames to engulf them or the skeleton to grab her. But nothing happened. The skeleton continued to stare off into the night, smiling at nothing, seeing only darkness.

Sandra pulled the bone away, and the skeleton shifted, knocking its skull against the side of the coffin. She backed away from the coffin until she bumped into Max. "Got it," she said.

He kissed her cheek. "Let's get out of here."

With large strides, they worked their way back to Leon and the boardwalk. Leon helped boost Sandra up. She, in turn, reached down and helped pull up Max. It took both of them to help Leon up.

Max shined his light in Leon's face. "Tell Mother Hope she can expect to hear from me in a few days. And I expect some answers."

A voice called out, "I think I can provide that. Oh, and I'll be taking the bone of Mr. Johnathan Shoemaker."

Max turned, already knowing who he would see. After all, he had heard that voice earlier that same day — Edward Wallace.

Chapter 7

FLANKED BY FOUR MEN wearing hooded robes, Edward blocked the way across the boardwalk. He had slicked his hair back for the evening and wore a dark suit with a clean, white vest. An ornate pendant hung around his neck. Looked rather like a vampire, though Max made sure to keep that thought quiet.

Unless vampires ...

He caught Sandra's eye. She shook her head slightly and mouthed *No such thing.* He offered a grin and a wink. To some that might have seemed like he said *Of course, I knew that* but just as Sandra knew his initial question from a glance, she would know he actually meant *Yes, I know we've talked about vampires in the past, but I needed the reassurance.*

Taking one step forward, Max said, "Edward Wallace, this is my wife Sandra."

"I already know her name. I do my research, too."

"Then you probably know Leon Moore, as well."

With a sneer, the tendons in Edward's neck pulled taut. "I have no fear of the Magi. Pathetic little group."

"Aren't you going to introduce your friends?"

He put out his hand and held it firm — not a trace of fear. "Give me that bone, and you can walk away unharmed."

Max felt Sandra's arm brush him as she placed the bone behind her back. He checked Leon — the man clenched his jaw while glowering across at Edward. Not good. With that kind of hatred seething out, things could go bad at any moment.

"Wait a minute," Max said, forcing levity into his voice. "You said you were going to give us answers first. Since the Magi here won't tell us anything, we'd like to know what we've stumbled into. Because let me tell you something I've learned over the years — once we get involved in this stuff, it won't leave us alone."

"I'm not surprised in the least." Edward lowered his hand. "People like Mother Hope want nothing more than to keep control over as many as they can. Especially if you're gifted."

"Are you gifted?"

"Aren't we all?"

Max stepped toward the railing while wagging a finger. "Good point." He had to keep talking while he searched for a way to get free. He trusted that Sandra also wracked her brain for a solution. Leon, however, continued to throw visual spears at Edward. Max went on, "You seem to know a bit about us. I'm guessing you found out quite a bit about our lives since we moved here."

"You're not exactly the quietest people."

"It's not our fault. The Magi, the Hulls — these groups keep bringing all of this nonsense to our doorstep. Often, we're not even given a choice."

"That's my exact point. Mother Hope controls you, forces you in a direction that you don't even understand. That's why you clamor for answers."

Rolling his fingers into fists, Leon said, "Stop talking about her."

Max stepped in front of Leon. "I still haven't gotten any answers, and you said you would provide them. So, how about it? What's with all these old skeletons?"

"Abagail. That's what this is all about."

"Who is she?"

"I've given you the answer because I think it's terrible the way the Magi play games with you. But you don't get to keep asking me questions. Now, give me that bone." Edward thrust his hand out once more.

Through grinding teeth, Leon said, "The Magi and Mother Hope don't mess with good people. They try to protect the world from bastards like you."

Edward closed his hand. "Mr. Moore, have you ever considered how old Mother Hope is?"

"Keep your mouth shut about her."

"No offense intended. I only wanted to make sure you understood the kind of person you work for. I mean she's old. Over a century. Not all of that time was spent with the Magi."

"I'm sure she's made her mistakes, but she's done more good fighting people like you."

"You don't know anything about me. How can you be so sure I'm the bad guy? Mother Hope has been around a long time. Long before the Civil Rights Movement. Long enough, in fact, that her views towards black men may not be all that enlightened. Do you know for a fact she's not the real enemy?"

Max couldn't understand why Edward provoked Leon, but he had no doubt it was a mistake. Leon's face tightened. Max stepped over to Sandra and whispered, "Get to our car and protect that bone."

They had been through enough together that Sandra didn't express worry or doubt. Those feelings reverberated through her, but she wouldn't protest. He only hoped she'd listen.

"Tell me," Edward went on, "does she call you by name or is just *boy?*"

"Bastard!" Leon charged forward with more strength than Max would have imagined. A year ago, Leon's old body had been stooped over and weak. The magic that kept Mother Hope alive for over a century clearly brought with it more than exterior youth. She had given Leon many of his years back, and he threw all those years into his fists as he barreled toward Edward.

The four hooded men rushed forward. This must have been part of their plan all along — they wanted to take out Leon. But from their action, they expected Max and Sandra to stand by, cowering like two pampered suburbanites. They were wrong.

As Leon threw his first punch, landing a solid hit upon the hooded man on the left, Max launched at the hooded man on the far right. A bit of a sucker punch, he fully admitted, but he never worried about fair play when it came to fighting for his life.

Max brought back his arm for a second strike and felt his elbow connect hard with another hooded man. Luck always played a part in a fight, and this time it played a helpful part. He punched forward.

Leon lifted one man into the air and tossed him over the railing. The man yelped, followed by a muddy splash and a dull grunt.

In a flash, Max connected with Sandra. He winked at her. "Ready?" He turned back and shoved Edward aside. Then he sprinted down the boardwalk.

"Get him!"

Max heard a delightful crack in Edward's voice. But seconds later, the rapid beats of men running on the boardwalk chased him further through the woods. With any luck, Max figured he pulled at least two of the men his way. Leon could handle the rest while Sandra escaped.

Checking behind him, Max failed to see one of the boards missing from the walk. His foot caught on the lip of the exposed board and down he went. He bounced into the hard walk and splinters dug into his hands as he skidded several feet.

He rolled onto his back. The good news — two men plus Edward approached him. The bad news — he didn't have time to get on his feet.

One man kept his hood drawn. The other shook his off revealing a thick, wide face and an eye patch over his right eye. Edward leaned against the wood railing and watched as his men punched Max in the stomach and kicked him in the sides.

"You know," Edward said as Eye-patch popped Max in the gut, "I had been told of your brazen stupidity." *Kick!* "You take wild risks that should've gotten you killed long ago." *Punch!* "But you're quite lucky apparently. Or perhaps you were protected by the Hulls back then." *Kick!* "Yet now, the Hulls are gone, and the only one who can protect you is Mother Hope." *Punch!* "But we both know that won't happen."

Max tried to lift his head but it might as well have been a ball of iron. The beating had stopped, but that only let his body change focus from enduring the hits to noticing the damage.

Pain throbbed along his right side.

The hooded man grabbed his arms and yanked him upward. He groaned as they shoved him against the railing opposite Edward. His head had started to lighten, at least. A few clean breaths of air, and he could stand on his own feet.

"You look awful," Edward said, and Eye-patch laughed in short, grunting bursts. Edward laced his fingers together and cracked his knuckles. He watched Max from the corner of his eye like a predator taking the measure of its prey.

But to Max, it felt rehearsed. The low jabs to his abdomen, however, felt quite authentic. "I have waited long enough," Edward said, punctuating with a punch. "Give me that bone."

Max's head lolled forward. "Can't do that."

"You will, or I'll beat you to death." Edward struck Max twice to underscore his point.

"Sorry, pal. I don't have it."

Edward's mouth dropped open as he realized his mistake. "The wife." He looked to his henchmen. "The wife has the bone."

Max felt the grip on his arms loosen and wasted no time taking advantage. He lunged forward, leading his shoulder straight into Edward's stomach. As the young man doubled-over with a hoarse cough, Max vaulted over the railing and into the woods.

Branches whipped by as he dashed through. He hopped across several wide stones to avoid a sodden section of land. The ground angled upward causing Max to slow his progress. Those hooded men had to be behind him, closing in, but he wouldn't make the same mistake twice. *Keep your eyes forward. Keep running.*

Max saw the woodchip path and followed it further up the hill. His legs burned. Gasping with each step, he came upon a shallow creek. He jumped across and headed straight off the path. Sweat soaked through his shirt as he slowed his pace.

He had to stop to catch his breath and get his bearings. The street noises sounded louder and he thought he glimpsed headlights spraying across the trees as a car turned onto the main road running alongside the park. Except it could also have been flashlights from his enemies.

No time to waste figuring it out. The fact that lights came from further upward convinced him that they belonged to cars. He took off, but between the beatings, the exertion of his initial escape, and his lack of regular exercise, Max had reached the limit of his running. He opted for a fast walk.

Not fast enough.

As he entered a narrow clearing marked with a circle of seven stones each the size of a small bed, Eye-patch appeared ahead. Max turned back but the man's hooded partner was there, breathing heavily but walking forward. In the center of the circle, Max spied a half-charred log. Too big to handle as a weapon, and too charred to hold together.

Off to the right, a third hooded man joined them. That didn't bode well for Leon. To the left, Max saw Edward. At least Max's vanity had some relief — sweat dribbled down Edward's face, too.

Max had expected Edward to say something snide or victorious. Instead, the man crossed his arms and watched as the hooded figures closed in. The assault began from behind — a kick to the back of the knees that sent Max crashing down. Like hungry wolves, the other two crowded in. Each took a turn striking Max while Edward looked on.

"Stop!" Sandra shouted, her voice deep and full of menace.

The men halted, curious at the sudden disturbance. With both hands, Sandra held the marked bone above her head. Her mouth moved, but Max could not make out the words — until he realized she was casting a spell.

"Be gone!" she yelled.

The bone glowed orange. Edward looked back at his men, saw the fear on their face, but before he could speak, bright white light flashed off the bone. It lit up the area like security lights flooding a parking lot. The men dropped Max. One pulled his hood further forward before rushing off down the hill. The other two stepped back. Eye-patch raised a hand over his eyes as he turned away. Max tried to stand but only managed to fall against one of the large stones.

Edward turned to his men. "Relax," he said. "It's nothing."

As Sandra concentrated on the bone, Edward strode right up to her and clocked her on the chin. Max winced, and Sandra let out a shocked cry. Max shoved off the stone, but two men grabbed him by the shoulders and held him back. It wasn't too hard — most of his strength had been beaten out of him.

Snatching the bone from the ground, Edward turned back. He crouched before Max, and with a condescending shake of his head, he placed his hand on Max's shoulder. "I don't care that you once fought the Hulls. I don't care that you've had some experience with magic. You're in over your head here. Please, for the sake of your wife, stop now. You tried, and you lost. I don't want to see you get hurt any worse, and if you get in our way again, you will be. A lot worse. You understand?"

Max nodded because he knew Edward needed some sort of response.

"Good. We're not out to harm anybody — well, not anybody innocent — and if you don't listen to me here, right now, you'll no longer be innocent." He put his forehead against Max's forehead. With a dead look in his eyes, he said, "I'm not interested in murdering you or your wife, but I'm not unwilling either. And you know we can hide a body. Look how long those coffins remained hidden."

He patted Max on the cheek and stood. With a motion of his head, the hooded men followed him as he walked on the park path. Max waited until the night covered the last trace of them. Then he stumbled over to Sandra.

"You okay?" he asked as he helped her sit up.

Dazed, she rubbed her jaw. "He hit me," she said, with a bit of surprise.

"You took it like a champ."

"Great. You can make a movie about me. Did he get the bone?"

"It's okay. Don't worry about it." Seeing she wasn't seriously injured, he dropped back against a tree. "What kind of spell was that?"

"Nothing, really. Just a light show. It doesn't really do anything. It's more of a beginner's exercise to try to focus energy."

"It was enough to save me. Thank you."

She leaned over to rest her head on his chest, but he recoiled. She tried to hold him, but he groaned. Finally, she stood and offered her hand. "How about I drive home?"

Chapter 8

WHEN MAX AWOKE, the sun had yet to rise. He felt worse than hungover — he felt like he had been beaten by a gang of hooded thugs. *Oh, wait.*

Careful not to disturb Sandra — her soft snores brought warmth to his heart before the bruises on his body whisked it away — Max slipped out of bed and crept downstairs to the kitchen. He shuffled across the tiled floor like an old man suffering from arthritis and bad joints and weak legs. Turning a dimmer knob, he brought up the over-the-sink lamp — enough light for him to see by but nothing bright and blinding so early in the morning.

As quietly as he could manage, he scooped coffee into a filter, placed the filter in the machine, and filled up the water. After turning it on, he leaned against the counter, crossed his arms, and pursed his lips. All he had done was make coffee, yet his muscles were already tired. The old body did not bounce back like it would have a few years ago.

A little coffee, some breakfast, and he should feel better. Not one-hundred-percent, but better.

How did this keep happening? How did they keep getting stuck in these situations? Having Mother Hope and the Magi take over should have been a step up from the Hulls, but at least with the Hulls, Max knew where to look for the double-crosses and outright lies. With Mother Hope, he had no idea what to expect.

"Morning, Max," Drummond said, rising up through the sink.

Max pulled a coffee mug from the cabinet. "What does it say about me that you don't even faze me anymore?"

"Really? I thought the sink thing was rather new."

"Maybe it's just too early for a reaction. Besides, after the night I had, I doubt I could muster the energy to be surprised."

Drummond looked Max up and down. "What happened to you?"

While sipping coffee and letting the caffeine boost do its trick, Max told Drummond all that had transpired. The part about Leon's fighting skills forced Drummond's begrudging acknowledgment. But when Max reached the point where Edward decked Sandra, Drummond's pale face burned.

"Bad enough this punk punched a lady, but he dared to punch our lady. Next time I see him, I promise we'll make this right."

Max's headache throbbed too much for more than swirling his coffee. "I don't even want to know what that means."

"It means he better watch his step 'cause he's got a ghost for an enemy."

"You be careful about that. I don't want you getting too riled up and then losing control. You know what could happen to you." Once before, Drummond's rage had taken over — nearly turned him into a poltergeist. "And I'd hate to have to fight you, too."

"Don't worry about me. I got myself under control. I know how far I can push it."

"You better." Max's stomach grumbled, but he ignored it. No good ever came to him from eating before sunrise. "Wait a second. The sun's not even up. What are you doing here?"

Drummond drifted backwards as if he needed to put a little distance between them. "Nothing. I mean I came to report in, but it can wait. Go back to sleep."

"You clearly don't have any big news to report. I know you. If you'd found something worth telling, you'd be bouncing around like a little kid. And you always wait until we're at the office for that kind of thing. What's going on?"

"Relax. There's no *anything* going on."

"Then why are you here?"

Drummond wiped his forehead. "Now don't get all upset. You've got healing to do. Besides, this is nothing. Honest."

"You know what I think when people tell me they're being honest."

"Look, all that's happening is that sometimes, on occasion, not often at all really, but sometimes I come by here in the morning or late at night to make sure you guys are safe, that's all."

"What? You're sneaking in here at night? Like a peeping Tom?"

"Hey, that's not it at all. I worry about you guys. That's it. You know, it isn't easy being a ghost, especially a P.I. ghost. Lots of people in the Other want to give up worrying about the law, so they don't take kindly to a guy like me. I don't make a lot of friends."

Max paused. "Wow, that was honest."

"I'm not trying to be a creep or anything like that. But since you got that curse on you and then we spent time together with you as a ghost, well, it got me thinking."

The curse, its mark on Max's chest — Max didn't like to think about it too often. But it was there within him, a grenade under his skin, ready for Mother Hope to pull the pin whenever she chose. "You're worried that we'll be killed, that we'll end up stuck as ghosts like you."

"I think if you get killed, you'll both move on with ease. And then that'll be it. I'll have nobody here to work with." Drummond raised his hands before Max could speak. "I know, I know. Eventually, you two are going to pass on. But that shouldn't be until you've lived a long, full life. So, if I have to come in here now and then to make sure everything is safe for you guys, I'm going to do it."

Max poured another cup of coffee — this would definitely be a two cup morning. "Okay, I guess. I suppose I should appreciate it."

"Do me a favor, though. Don't tell Sandra. I think it'll bother her."

"You think?" Max took a deep breath to stop from raising his voice. "Let's talk about something else. Tell me what you found in the Other. I'm guessing still no Archibald

Henderson."

Latching onto work, Drummond returned to his usual strong demeanor. "He's long gone. In fact, most of them are. Turns out the Other has a limit to how long you can stay. Most ghosts that hang around are waiting for some sort of closure from their lives. When that happens, they move on. But some either can't accept their deaths and stay or, like me, choose to stay for some other reasons. Well, the Other doesn't like that. So, according to the old timers I could find, the Other will force ghosts to move on if they've been around for over two hundred years. It's important, too, because if that didn't happen, the Other would be overcrowded with ghosts — and it's plenty crowded as it is."

"Are you saying that any ghost from the time of the Revolution is gone?"

"Most are. But however the Other operates, it isn't perfect. It misses some of the ghosts, or maybe whatever allows it to force ghosts to move on is slightly selective. I don't know. But there are a handful of ghosts that are still hanging around. Maybe about one percent. Of course, if you think about how many people have died over the last thousand years, one percent is a lot."

"Then there are people from the Revolution?"

"Heck, there's a lady from 1502, so yeah, there's a bunch from the Revolution, but not nearly enough to make it likely we'll get anything worthwhile."

"So, you got nothing."

Wagging a finger, Drummond grinned. "Do I ever let you down? I found one guy who claims he fought the British during the war. Says he's from North Carolina and that he could help us out. I don't trust what he's saying entirely, but I don't know my history well enough to tell for sure. I figured I could bring him in, we'll chat, and maybe we luck into something useful."

Max nodded. "Set it up."

"Who are you talking to?" Mrs. Porter said as she walked into the kitchen. She wore a floral housecoat that draped the tiles.

"Just myself," Max said.

"Be careful about that. Wouldn't want people thinking you're losing your marbles." She tittered at her own joke. "How about I make you an egg sandwich?"

Drummond clapped his hands together once. "I'll get that guy right away. Enjoy your breakfast. I don't need to be watching food. That never goes well for me."

Max couldn't respond, and Drummond knew it. The ghost opted for a simple wave good-bye and disappeared through a wall. Mrs. Porter dug out a pan and clanked it onto the stovetop.

"Easy, Mom. Sandra's still asleep."

"An egg sandwich was always your favorite growing up. No butter on the toast, though. I remember that. Do you? Probably not — you were so little."

Max watched as she cracked two eggs into a small bowl. He had seen her do this so many times, and the sound instantly brought him back to the breakfast table in Michigan. "I remember," he said. "The first egg sandwich you ever made me, you asked if I wanted butter on the toast."

"You said you wanted gobs of butter. On both sides of the toast."

"I loved that word back then — gobs. I'd find any excuse to use it."

"I was a good mother. I warned you that it would be messy that way, but you didn't want to listen to anything I had to say. So, you got your gobs." She set two pieces of bread in the toaster and poured the beaten eggs into the hot pan.

The corners of Max's mouth rose as he pictured that day. Sitting at the table, his chin resting on his hands as his mother placed the egg sandwich on his plate. For some reason that particular morning, he was famished. He grabbed that sandwich and never took a bite.

"I can still feel it today," he said with a snort. "Butter all over my fingers and my palms, and even a bit ran down toward my elbow."

"After that, you never wanted butter on your toast. But I

give you lots of credit — especially because you were willing to try it again without the butter." She placed the completed egg sandwich on a plate and handed it to him. "And you've loved them ever since."

"Thanks, Mom." He kissed her cheek before taking his plate to the table.

"Well, it's not like I ever expect you to listen to your mother. But it's nice to know that you come around to trust me once-in-a-while."

Max picked up his sandwich and held it near his mouth. He tried to ignore the unsubtle comment, tried to focus on the simple pleasure of an egg sandwich, but he set it back on the plate. "Something bothering you?"

"Me? Not at all. I'm here visiting my wonderful son and his wife. Why should I be bothered? Here I am, getting to spend time with you, and it's barely even morning. I'm dog-tired, but a mother has to do these things sometimes in order to see her child."

"You didn't have to get up special for me."

"When else was I going to see you?"

"Well, maybe if you had given us some warning you were coming, we could have cleared our schedule so that you wouldn't be stuck."

"Who's stuck? Your employee, J, is a lovely boy. I really like him. We had a great time together."

Max couldn't tell if she was being sarcastic or serious. "I'm glad you two get along. And I'm sorry I haven't been available yet. I didn't expect to be working a case so soon after ..."

"After what?"

Rubbing the mark on his chest, Max said, "After our last case. But business is good, and you always told me that you should never back away from good business."

Mrs. Porter lifted her chin, and Max thought she might storm out of the room — she never liked having her words thrown back at her. "I'm glad your work is going so well, but that doesn't change the fact that I'm your mother. Aren't you the boss? Can't you decide to take the day off to spend a smidge of time with me? After all, I came a long way to be here."

"I promise we will get time together, but it's not all that simple. I am the boss, but I have responsibilities, too."

"I flew in a plane to get here. Do you know how much I hate flying?"

"We went to Disney in Orlando when I was seven. I think you screamed more than the infants on the plane."

Max hoped his humor would ease her, but his mother's eyes widened. "Don't you get fresh with me. I deserve some respect here."

"I'm sorry. I was only trying to —"

"I know exactly what you were trying to do. Your old mother isn't an idiot. You clearly don't have time for me, and you don't want to make time. My ticket home isn't for a few more days. I'll try my best to stay out of your way."

Though he wanted to remain calm, he couldn't hide the way his jaw set in frustration. "Stop it. Please. I promised you that we'd get together and we will." Max had an idea — one he recognized as a bad idea from the start, but at that moment, any solution sounded good to his ears. "How about we have lunch today? I'll take you to a nice place. Real special. I'll figure a way to rearrange my schedule."

"You don't have to trouble yourself."

"I want to. I'll get Sandra to cover my workload. And I'll take you to the Green Valley Grill. We'll have to leave a little early because the place is in Greensboro. About thirty or forty minutes from here, but it'll be worth it."

Though she was unwilling to smile, Max's mother did sit a bit straighter in her chair. "I think that sounds lovely. The Green Valley Grill? What kind of food is that?"

"All sorts of stuff. Fancy stuff. You'll love it." He could feel the guilt rising in him, but he pushed on. "The restaurant is attached to this old hotel. It's a charming place, beautifully built. The O. Henry Hotel — after the writer."

He picked up his sandwich and forced a bite down his throat. He wasn't sure which caused his food to stick more —

using his mother as cover for a visit to the Magi headquarters or knowing that he planned to confront Mother Hope while there.

Probably both.

Chapter 9

THE GREEN VALLEY GRILL had a high, vaulted ceiling that covered the square dining room like an atrium. A healthy mixture of wood and stone decorated the square dining room. Sunlight broke through with a bright, airy feel as if the restaurant had been intended for a social meeting of academics — much like a modern library.

Mrs. Porter was happy. Max saw it in the excited way she had clucked about the house before they left, the way she chattered along as they drove to Greensboro, and the way she grew silent upon taking her seat as if they had entered a place of reverence instead of consumption.

"Are you sure you can afford this?" she asked when she looked over the menu.

"Don't worry about it," he said, and for an instant, a flare of pride ignited in his chest. But that made him think of the mark of his curse, and that made him think of Mother Hope.

She would not be happy to see him — especially since Edward Wallace had escaped with the bone. Though perhaps Mother Hope had taken out her anger on Leon. If Max had any luck, she would be tuckered out and willing to talk. Max never had that kind of luck, though.

They ordered their food — chorizo burger for Max, baked pecan encrusted trout for his mother — and watched as a young couple with an infant settled in at a table nearby. Mrs. Porter's face lit up as she twinkled her fingers at the baby.

She sighed. "I suppose I should give up praying for a grandchild."

That snapped Max back from thinking about Mother Hope. "I thought we were trying to have a nice lunch."

"What's not nice about children?"

"Are you really going to pretend you don't know what you said? Nothing's changed for us. Sandra and I are not having children. We've got a busy, full, and fulfilling life down here, and I'm fairly certain a child would ruin that."

"Okay. You don't have to get bent out of shape." She placed her napkin on her lap with sharp motions. "You two don't want children, don't have children. That's your business. I don't need to be consulted about it. If you think it's best not to continue the Porter bloodline, then so be it."

"Please, Mom. Don't start this again."

"I'm not starting anything. I'm merely pointing out that should anything happen to you, that's it for our family name. You act like you're indestructible, but you're like the rest of us. You can get hurt, too."

Max wanted to lift his shirt, let her see all the bruising from the previous night's excursion, but that would only have frightened her and led to endless questions. He would have had to explain about the skeleton and the hooded men, how they chased him down and beat him, and how through it all, he feared he would not live or worse, that they might hurt Sandra. Worried he might start to shake, maybe even cry, he shoved his thoughts away.

"I do not think I'm indestructible," he said. "But I know I can't go through life afraid to take a risk."

"That's not what I'm saying. I'm talking about the fact that life is unexpected. You can plan for things to be a certain way, aim for a prized job or plan for a specific career, but in the end, life does what it wants. You don't get a say. Take your father — we never planned for him to die so young. I always thought he and I would grow old together. Frankly, I figured I'd be the one to die first. But that's not the way life happened."

Max twisted up inside. He tried to be angry at his mother for harping on the children issue, but bringing up his father quelled him. At the same time, he kept thinking about Mother Hope. He shouldn't have set this lunch up — it wasn't fair to his mother.

"Oh, just ignore me," Mrs. Porter said, forcing her lips

upward as she shooed him off with her hands. "I'm an old woman. I don't understand the way you kids do things, but that doesn't mean much. It's part of life, isn't it? That children grow to stand up against their parents' wishes. It's normal."

Max made a fist and bumped it lightly on the edge of the table. "I'm not trying to stand up to you or cause you any stress or anything like that." He closed his eyes, only for a second, but his mind jumped through a few hoops to arrive at a simple decision — Mother Hope could wait. "You know what we should do? Finish our lunch, and go for a stroll or maybe you'd like to catch a movie. Something together like that."

"Don't you have to get back to work?"

"Sandra's got it covered. Besides, I know she'll be happy to take on extra work if it means you and I can spend more time together."

His mother placed her hands in her lap. When she lifted her head, she had a warm smile. It took Max a second to realize that her gaze actually went above him. A man with no neck and a thick, bald head leaned over. Though drenched in cologne, the well-dressed man could not hide the sour stench of old alcohol on his breath.

"Excuse me, but a business associate of yours would like a word," the man said.

Max shook his head — happy that the rest of him did not start shaking, too. "You'll have to extend my apologies. Please tell her I'm here with my mother, and I'll call her later tonight."

The man stammered before saying, "I can't do that. You have to come with me."

"Look, I told you already —"

"It's okay," Mrs. Porter said. "I don't mind waiting a bit, if you have important business to take care of." To the Magi thug, she added, "Would you be kind enough to send somebody over with a dessert tray? I'm feeling adventurous."

The thug put a big paw on Max's arm. "I'll make sure they come by. Get whatever you want. It'll be our treat."

"Why, thank you." She brightened — no doubt impressed that Max's worthless research firm wasn't so worthless.

Max stood. "I'll only be a few minutes." Before she muttered something along the lines of *Take your time*, he turned to the thug. "After you."

He followed the big man through the restaurant toward the bar which connected with the O. Henry Hotel. This had been the route Max had planned to sneak his visit to Mother Hope, but now he didn't need an excuse. His mother had handed him over without a thought.

Walking into the hotel's main lobby, Max noticed only a heavyset woman manning the reception desk — new employee since the last time he had been here. The dark woods and subdued atmosphere closed in as he processed the idea that Mother Hope had sent for him. She knew he was at the restaurant which suggested that she had the hotel under surveillance — not surprising since the Magi were headquartered here but disturbing nonetheless.

The thug pointed to the sitting area, an open section much like the restaurant with a high-ceiling, and said, "Sit."

Max obeyed while the man went to the front desk and whispered to the new employee. Overstuffed couches and stiff chairs crowded the sitting area. Along the walls near the ceiling ran O. Henry's most famous story, "The Gift of the Magi". Though this particular representation of the story contained a spell to protect the hotel, Max did not feel too protected.

The man returned, clutched onto Max's bicep, and pulled him to his feet. "You do what I say and you stay quiet. Got it?"

"Sure."

The grip on his arm tightened. "I said to stay quiet. Right?"

Max nodded. Despite the man's bulk, he moved with the grace of a boxer — easily navigating Max through the maze of chairs and coffee tables until they reached the faux-gold elevator doors opposite the front desk. While maintaining his hold on Max's arm, the man placed a key into the elevator panel. A moment later, the elevator doors opened.

They stepped in, and Max focused on what he would say to Mother Hope when he reached her penthouse office. But the bald thug extended his thick finger and pressed for the basement. Max's stomach dropped with the elevator.

As they lowered beyond the floors marked on the elevator panel, Max turned all his energy on keeping his composure. He had been down here before. He had been tortured here. But if he started panicking, the outlook would be grim.

Keep it together. Keep it together.

The doors slid open to a long hall. "Come on," the man said, and yanked Max along. They stopped at the first door on the left.

"No," Max said. He couldn't stop himself. "You don't have to put me in there. Whatever I did to piss off Mother Hope, just tell me, and I'll make sure it doesn't happen again."

The man pushed Max into the room — a stark, empty room with a large mirror on one wall as if this were a police interrogation room. Except instead of a table in the middle, iron rings had been bolted into the wall. The man used handcuffs to lock Max's wrists to the rings.

"Hold on," the man said, leaning his neckless head closer. "Are you crying?"

Max never felt the tears form, but once pointed out, he felt the trickle down his cheek. Tears or not, he boiled at the sound of disgust in the man. "What do you care? You've delivered me here. Go tell Mother Hope she can send those two bastards to work me over."

A sadistic grin lifted the man's lips, revealing yellowed teeth. "No, they already had their turn with you before. I'm up now."

"You guys are taking turns?"

"You've done damage to Mother Hope. We all want our chance to do some damage to you."

A hard, strong voice called out from the doorway. "That's enough, Trevor."

The short woman shuffling in looked frail. She walked with an ivory-tipped cane and hunched over through each step. Her gray hair poked out from beneath a series of scarves that, along with her numerous rings and necklaces, lent her the image of an old gypsy. Mother Hope. Head of the Magi group and one of the most powerful witches in all of North Carolina —

perhaps, in all of the United States.

Trevor — boy, that thick-bodied bruiser did not look like a Trevor — bowed his head as he backed up two steps. "I didn't do anything to him, Ma'am. Not yet."

Mother Hope moved in close to Max and stared straight into his eyes. "You shouldn't be here."

Max shrugged and his chains rattled. "I had some questions about the case."

"That's what Leon is for."

"He couldn't provide the answers."

"Then you find them out on your own. You do not come here." With the end of her cane, she tapped the mark on his chest. "I would've thought you understood the danger of visiting me — especially unannounced."

Shaking his handcuffed hands, Max said, "Believe me, I don't like coming here either, but if you're going to force us to work for you, then you're going to have to help us function. Standing in our way only leads to bad situations."

"I don't care about your excuses. You've been assigned a task —"

"Which you are withholding information about. Look, we just spent several years under the thumb of the Hull family. You see how that turned out for them. Much of their mess could have been avoided if they had been straight with me from the start. Don't make that same mistake."

"The Hulls failed because they kept secrets from each other in the family and because they failed to listen to their trusted advisors. You are neither my family nor a trusted advisor."

Trevor giggled — a disturbing sound from one so large. Mother Hope glared at him until he quieted down.

Max hoped to catch her off guard while she dealt with Trevor. "What's with the bones? What's the curse? And how did Leon know where the second body was? What's really going on here?"

But Mother Hope merely shook her head. "You are nothing to me but a hired researcher. It is not important nor necessary that you understand why I have an assignment for you. It is only necessary that you complete the assignment. How I come to my information is equally not your concern."

She pulled loose one of her many necklaces. This one, an Ankh, had been made of bone and threaded through a smooth, thin rope. "I made this the very night we destroyed the Hulls," she said and held it close to Max's face. "I made it from shards of Dr. Connor's skull that I found stuck to my clothing."

Dr. Connor had been the Hull family witch. After her death, her skull was cursed, muting her ability to cast spells from the ghost world. Part of defeating the Hulls involved destroying that skull. To see that some of it, no matter how small, had survived, burned Max's throat with bile.

Dangling the bone Ankh before him, she said, "You have no concept of what I can do with an object like this. I have held back from casting my magic against you in any serious manner because you and your wife have been useful to me. Do not start thinking you know how strong I am. And certainly don't start thinking you can beat me. I am not like the Hulls. I've not been lulled by centuries of dominance into believing I am invincible. I know I can be hurt. So I pay close attention to those around me. I know where my enemies are."

"You think I'm your enemy?" Max said, the words stumbling out of his throat.

She snatched the Ankh back to her chest, looping the rope over her head. "I'm not sure, yet. I know you don't approve of me, and I believe you would have been happy to see me destroyed alongside the Hulls. But I wonder if that's enough to make you a true enemy. You should hope not. Because I think you value your wife more than all else. That's your weakness."

"It's my strength."

"You're act of continuing to stay in Winston-Salem and working for me must be to appease her. That's sweet but stupid. It's also keeping you alive. Because I think you're still useful and that I can still control you. Proof is in the fact that you willfully came down here and allowed Trevor to cuff you to the wall. Proof is in the fact that when you leave this building with no better answers than you entered, you'll still work for me — even after I have you beaten."

"Aw, come on." Max kicked the wall with his heel.

Mother Hope headed out. At the door, without turning back, she said, "Not in the face. Nobody should see the bruises."

"Yes, ma'am," Trevor said.

Max's face scrunched up as he held back the urge to weep. Once Mother Hope left, Trevor moved in, his wide mouth open like a fish as he tightened a fist.

"Wait, wait," Max said. "Don't hit my right side. I was in a fight last night. You hit me there and you'll break my ribs."

"You don't get to tell me where to hit you."

"Didn't you hear Mother Hope? She said nobody should see the bruises you give me. You think breaking my ribs won't be noticeable?"

Despite his thick-headed appearance, Trevor displayed true brains. He paused, considered, and then pulled Max's shirt up. With a long whistle, Trevor let the shirt drop.

"You're not good at fighting."

"I was jumped by three guys," Max said. "A big guy like you might be able to handle that, but I'm not a big guy."

He gazed upon Max with pity, but then opted to step toward Max's left side.

"You should've kept your mouth shut like I said. Mother Hope don't like people questioning her."

"So I'm learning."

The beating wasn't so bad — or perhaps having his body bashed up the night before had changed his perspective on levels of pain. It helped that Trevor's enthusiasm had waned after seeing Max's damaged torso. When it ended, Trevor eased Max out of the handcuffs and assisted him back into the elevator. Once in the main lobby, he took Max to a restroom.

Watching Max in the mirror, Trevor said, "Do yourself a favor — don't mess with Mother Hope. She'll destroy you." He gave Max a gentle pat on the back and walked out.

Max ran the water and cupped his hands under the spout. He wanted to rinse his face, but his hands were shaking. The beating itself could have been far worse, but his mind whirled around what it all meant for his future.

Mother Hope had a vicious streak in her that dug deep and ran blood-red. The Hulls had been powerful, but they had become complacent in their position. Mother Hope wanted to be clear that she would not be so easy to work with — and Max got the message.

He splashed water on his cheeks and rubbed his eyes. Patting his face dry with a paper towel, he took three deep breaths. He and Sandra had pushed through so much crap in the past. Mother Hope and the Magi were simply more obstacles. That's all.

Besides, unlike the Hulls, the Magi fought for the people. They wanted to prevent the abuses of magic the Hulls fostered. Mother Hope's methods were certainly harsh, but perhaps he should see it from her point of view.

She had a lot to contend with. Running any organization would be difficult, but running a group of spies, muscle men, and witches would take a disciplinary hand. Add to the mix a guy like Edward Wallace, and Mother Hope had to be more of a General during wartime than a benevolent leader of peace.

"Okay," Max said as he headed back to the restaurant. Though his sides ached, he actually felt better overall. The Magi were tough, but he could find a safe balance with them. After all, they had at least one goal in common — to stop people from using magic to cause harm.

He checked his watch — he had been gone almost twenty-five minutes. No doubt, his mother had worked herself into a froth of indignation. And they had a forty minute drive home.

Bracing himself for the verbal attack, he walked toward their table. A woman sat with his mother, the two chatting like old friends.

Max's skin turned to ice.

Mother Hope sat with his mother. The old witch had a hand on his mother's forearm, confiding something in a whisper that sent both ladies giggling.

"Oh, Max," his mother said with the joy of a teen going to her first prom. "I want you to meet this lovely lady. She has an unusual name, but don't let that fool you. She's down-to-Earth and a pure delight."

Mother Hope turned in her chair and offered a hand. "It's nice to meet you. Your mother is the true delight here."

Max hesitated, considered refusing her hand, but then saw the way his mother stared at him. She would be mortified if he acted rudely, and he would be forced to explain who Mother Hope really was — which only would lead to a discussion of ghosts and witches. That was not a conversation he welcomed.

Shaking her hand, he said, "Thank you. My mother is indeed delightful."

"I'm sure you value her greatly and only want the best things for her." Her grip tightened — not painfully so, but enough to show her intent. Her cold glare underscored her words. "You be a good boy and work hard, and I'm sure she'll live a long and healthy life."

Max let go of the hand and forced a pleasant demeanor. His heart hammered as all thoughts of understanding and balance and excuses for the Magi's behavior rushed out of his head. This woman would have made a great Mafia don.

"Don't worry," he said. "I'll take good care of her."

Mother Hope got to her feet. "Mrs. Porter, it's been a pleasure, but I'm sure your son has important work to get done, and I have my own appointments to keep. Enjoy the rest of your visit, and I hope we can chat again sometime."

"I'd love that," Max's mother said.

It took all of Max's remaining strength not to scream.

Chapter 10

MAX TRAMPLED A CLEAR PATH across the bedroom carpeting while Sandra brushed her teeth in the adjoining bathroom. After lunch with his mother and a nerve-wracked drive home, he had spent several hours in the office with his head buried in research. When he finally got home, Sandra had to know something went wrong, but she gave him the space he needed to cool down.

Luckily, Drummond had not returned from his latest foray into the Other. Max loved that old ghost, but he couldn't bear the thought of dealing with Drummond's guaranteed, hot-headed reaction to Mother Hope's actions. Plus, if Drummond had returned, it would mean moving the case forward, and Max didn't know how he felt about that.

"Which is part of my problem with all this," he said to Sandra as he started another circuit around the bedroom. Only after he had showered and dressed for bed, only after Sandra had started her nighttime routine, did he finally have the ability to open up about what had happened. "Maybe we've finally reached the point where we're truly in this too deep. I mean it's one thing to fight the Hulls from within — we were really just trying to free ourselves from a bad situation — but in this case, heck, we don't even really know what the case is all about."

"We've been involved in worse."

"And where did that get us? PB is still recovering from being shot, and he's just a kid." Max froze. "Where's J? Have you seen him today?"

"He's fine. He spent most of the day playing nurse to PB, and I set him up on an air mattress in your office. I don't think he wants to be alone in his apartment. Once PB is healthy enough to return, J will go back, too. For now, though, there's no need for him to sleep on the couch again."

Sandra entered the bedroom and pulled back the comforter on the bed. Max had no intention of getting into bed. He couldn't stop moving.

"I'm glad J's fine, but that's part of this mess, isn't it? I shouldn't have to worry about the Sandwich Boys. They shouldn't be getting so close to the danger in our line of work."

"Hon, sit." Sandra patted a spot next to her. He did so, and she kissed his temple and hugged his shoulder. He tried not to wince. "Our business involves risk. You know that better than any of us. Look at all the bruises on your body. PB and J both have been working with us enough to know about those risks. Besides, they're tough. They've lived harder lives than you or me."

"I know. It's not right, though. We shouldn't have to keep fighting this kind of thing."

"What? Magic and witches?"

"All of it. I thought with the Hulls gone, these problems would settle down. I'm not stupid. I didn't think they'd disappear entirely, but shouldn't they have become — I don't know — less?"

Sandra laced her fingers through his and leaned her head on his shoulder. "We'll figure this out. You know that. We always do. And you know exactly how we're going to do it, too."

He couldn't hold back a smile. "Push straight on through."

"Damn right."

Man, he loved that woman. "Okay."

"We keep at it until we win."

"Right on, Coach."

"Good," she said, and Max thought she was going to turn in for a deep kiss — one that would lead them to a more intimate evening. Instead, her brow tightened and her playful smile drifted into a serious expression. "I have an idea of where to start."

"I don't like the sound of that."

"Really? I haven't even said anything yet, and you're going to start doubting me?"

Max raised his hands in surrender. "Sorry. I've been through a lot today."

Softer, she said, "See that? You're handling it all so well, I forgot what happened to you." She clasped his hand again. "Okay. Here it is: I think we should take what we know, especially what I know about the writing on the bone, and we take it to a witch. Get an expert to tell us what's going on."

"A witch? What witch? They're practically extinct around here. We've known less than a handful — and that includes your limited dabbling and a coven of dead witches."

"But you were beaten up today by the Magi."

"What does that have to do with it?"

Like a teacher with enormous patience, she said, "The Hulls were ousted from their power only a short time ago. That's not enough time for any one group to fill the vacuum. Mother Hope and the Magi can't be the only ones. You think it's a coincidence that they suddenly have a case for us, that they strong arm you this way, or that some fool like Edward Wallace appears on the scene out of nowhere?"

"You're saying we're in the middle of a power struggle."

"Absolutely. I don't how these dead guys from the 1700s are connected, but you better believe they are. If I've learned anything from you and Drummond these past years, it's that there are no coincidences."

She was right — like usual — but that didn't make the idea of visiting a witch any more palatable. "Even if I wanted to take what we have to a witch, we don't know anyone other than your friend, Maria, and you're not in the best place with her. Heck, if you were, she probably would still refuse us after everything we put her through on our last case."

"I'll find somebody new to talk with. The Hulls are gone, nobody is in control yet, so the witches don't have to hide like before. They don't have to go through Dr. Connor or anybody before casting a powerful spell. It's open season out there."

Max popped to his feet. "That doesn't make me feel any better."

"I don't mean it like that. Do you see witchcraft shootouts

going on? No. I simply mean we can have a witch on our side, casting spells if we need, and nobody'll be looking over our shoulder. The witches are coming out, and we can use them to learn about that bone."

"Great — first, Dr. Connor, then Mother Hope, and now mystery witch. In case you forgot, I don't have a good history with witches."

"You've done fine with me."

"You're not a witch."

"Not yet."

Max dropped by her side, on his knees, his hands locked on either side of her. He had never sounded so cold in his life. "You listen to me. It's one thing to learn some basic spells to help us fight that world. It's another thing to start studying it to become a witch. A real witch. I mean, we've called you that before, but I never meant it like I think you're starting to."

"I can be a good witch. I don't have to learn the dark stuff."

"You really think you're the first to say that? We've been warned about witchcraft and we've both seen what can happen. Look at how it ruined Dr. Connor."

She took Max's face in her hands, and with a placating tone, she said, "Stop worrying. I am not an evil person, I am not working for the Hulls, and I am not Dr. Connor. If — and I'm saying *if* — I choose to study witchcraft further than the basics, then I promise you, I'll do it responsibly. In the meantime, we have a case to solve, and we're going to need a witch's help."

Max let out a sigh. He had said all he could. If he tried to "lay down the law" and forbid her from delving further into witchcraft, she would laugh at him — after she slapped his face and screamed bloody murder at him for an hour. She had heard his concerns, and he trusted she would do her best to keep them in mind as she pushed on.

In the end, he knew she was right about it all. They needed her to learn what she could on witchcraft. They needed to push through like they had done so in the past. They needed each other to be on the same side. And, for now, they needed a witch.

"One more thing," she said, unable to mask the hesitancy in her voice.

"What now?"

"Your mother."

"What about her?"

"She needs to go home."

Max's face dropped open. "You know I can't ask her to do that. She just got here. Besides, I thought I'd done a good job of keeping her out of your hair."

"This isn't about me, and you know it. Look at the argument we just had. Look at the bruises on your body. Look at the people we're talking about. Hulls and Magi and Mother Hope, not to mention Drummond — how are you going to explain any of that to your mother?"

"Why does she have to know about anything?"

"She doesn't. That's my point. Send her home, promise to visit in a few months, and you don't have to worry about her getting involved. But the longer she stays here, the more chances she has of bumping into things. What if J accidentally says something? What if she snoops around your desk one afternoon?"

"She's not a snooper."

"If she finds out any of what we do, if she learns that you talk to a ghost, she's liable to think you've lost your mind and have you committed."

Max turned to the bedroom door. "I can't believe you're asking me to turn my own mother away."

"Don't be dramatic. You know I'm not like that."

He turned back, his anger rising even while he knew she had a point. His mother would be better off back home, and their chaotic lives would be simpler to handle. But after all the times they had ignored her efforts to visit, the fact that it got to the point where she showed up unannounced, Max had to admit that he felt guilty. Guilt mixed with anger — not a good combination.

"I am not telling my mother she's not welcome here. You two have never liked each other, and that's fine. But don't put me in the middle of it."

"This has nothing to do with that."

"Of course it does. Anything involving my mother causes you to stiffen up. You act uncomfortable in your own house, uncomfortable around me, and you find every excuse to be somewhere else."

"It's not like that," she said, but she rolled her shoulders in an attempt to relax her stiffened back.

Max tried to ease back his voice. "Look, it's okay. I'm not suggesting you have to become buddies, and I don't mind playing interference for you. But it's not fair for you to insist that I send her home when she just got here. It's not right."

Sandra jumped to her feet, turned toward the bed, and punched her pillow. "You're not listening. I'm not saying any of that."

"Then what?"

When she turned back, her eyes blazed. "Forget it. You do what you want." She stormed into the bathroom and slammed the door shut.

Max slouched, stunned by the sudden end to their argument. That wasn't how things usually went between them in a fight. Normally, they would keep at it until they worked through the problem. Then they made up with a kiss and often a trip to bed. It was a pattern of behavior that Sandra had broken, and Max's stomach twisted at the sound of the bathroom fan whirring away — a sound, he suspected, meant to mask her anger or her tears.

That didn't go well, he thought as he stepped into the hall — no reason to force his wife's isolation in the bathroom. Once she realized he had left, she would at least have the bedroom to pace. He went downstairs, intending to get a glass of water — all that yelling had dried out his throat — but then he heard his mother and J talking in the office.

He stopped at the kitchen entrance. With his office adjacent, they would see him the moment he passed through the kitchen, and from their tones, he didn't want to intrude.

"I worry about him," J said. "He's been through a lot."

Max turned to go back upstairs, but he stayed still.

"Of course, you worry," Mrs. Porter said. "We all worry for those we care about. It's natural."

"PB's been my friend for a long time. I mean I know I'm young and all, but that don't mean he isn't close to me. You know?"

"I do."

"When I found out that bullet hit him, I didn't know what I'd do. And if he had died —"

"Then you'd carry on. That's what good people do. Death happens, but there's nothing honorable in killing yourself because your friend died."

Max heard the shock in J's voice. "No, no. That's not what I meant. I'd never off myself. But if something happened to PB, I'd seriously think about offing the bastard who dared —"

"Watch your mouth," Mrs. Porter snapped, and Max cringed as if she would reach out to slap him upside the head.

"Yes, ma'am. Sorry."

"J, whenever someone we love is hurt, we all feel the desire to defend our loved one or to have revenge. But that never works. If you ever lose PB, don't go that route. You have to suck up the pain and move on." She gave a knowing chuckle. "There's an old saying that the best revenge is to live well. That's what you do — live well."

"Is that what you're doing?"

There was a lengthy pause. Max thought he could hear his mother's soft gulp. "What do you mean?" she said.

"Hey, I thought we were being honest here. Just because Max is too busy to see what's going on, doesn't mean I can't see it. Tell me what happened."

"It's not like that. I'm not seeking revenge. But I am trying to live well, to keeping living on."

"You lost someone?"

"I did," Mrs. Porter said, and Max reached for the wall to steady himself. "It's no fun getting old. The world changes around you, and for a while, while you're still young, you can keep up with the changes. But that next generation is nipping at your heels, and the next thing you know, nothing is done the way it was when you were growing up. Everything seems wrong, and you fear for the future because those idiot kids can't possibly run the world successfully — not with their crazy, unrealistic ideas. Of course, the generation before mine thought the same thing.

"The worst part of getting old, though, is that all your friends get old, too. And then they start to go away. One by one, year after year, until you're living alone in a cold, rural town in Michigan, and you have only one friend left.

"Her name was Deena Hart. She moved to Michigan after her husband died because her children lived nearby. We met one afternoon at a charity drive for the fire department. One of those chicken dinner things. Anyway, you'll see when you're my age — you go to a function and there's somebody with as many wrinkles as you, and you instantly want to see if there's a friendship to be had because nobody else shares the frame of reference you have for anything. And we clicked — same tastes in music and movies, both of us loved to read, and we both indulged each other in getting drunk and reminiscing about our dead husbands."

Max bent over and tried to breathe slowly, but each time he imagined the scene his mother portrayed, he felt sharp pains in his lungs. How many times had she called him and he brushed her off? How many times had those calls been the desperate cry of his lonely mother?

J said, "So you two hooked up?"

"What? No. I'm not like that." Max expected his mother to launch into a lecture that J would never forget — not because of its coherence but because of its vehemence. Instead, she made a soft, thoughtful sound. "You prove my point."

"I did?"

"Your question about me and Deena — somebody from my generation or older would never ask such a thing. Most wouldn't even consider the possibility. But your generation has less of a problem with gay people. See? Times change.

"Anyway, no, we were not lovers. We were just two old ladies who enjoyed each other's company and felt lucky for it. We knew we had nobody else."

"She's gone now, right?"

"Two weeks ago. Heart attack. She had just been to the doctor, too — got a clean bill of health. But at our age, what can you do? We don't live forever."

"So you came here to be with your family. That's nice."

"I don't think my son feels the same. Certainly, not his wife." With an exhausted huff, she said, "I don't know what I'm going to do next, though. I suppose I'll go back home. For a little, at least. See if I can find a new friend."

"Pick a younger one."

Mrs. Porter laughed. "I'll try to remember that. But who knows? Maybe I'll sell my house and travel. I never saw as much of the world as I wanted."

"Or maybe you can stay here. I sure would like that."

"You're sweet. But I don't feel so welcome here."

Max hurried back to the stairs. Tears dampened his cheeks. Halfway up, he stopped. Sandra would be in no mood for another conversation that might devolve into a fight. He turned back and stopped. He should not have eavesdropped in the first place, and he wasn't sure he could handle hearing anything more. He looked upstairs, then down. Finally, he sat on the lip of one stair and leaned his head against the banister.

Chapter 11

THE NEXT MORNING STARTED EARLIER than Max had wanted. Sandra nudged his shoulder before dawn, rousing him from an uncomfortable night on the couch, and informed him that she had arranged a meeting with a witch in Lexington. She had the coffee ready when he finished his shower. Lest he think things were okay between them, her mouth never rose above a thin, straight line. Not that he felt all that forgiving either.

As they left, Max jotted a quick note to his mother. He promised to take her for a better lunch later in the day, and that with any luck, he would be able to carve out a full day soon. He taped the note to the coffee machine and headed out.

Driving down Route 52, Max and Sandra kept quiet. The radio remained off. Only the tires rumbling along the highway made any sound.

"Are you two sleepy or fighting?" Coming from the back seat, Drummond's voice jolted Max.

"Sheesh, you trying to kill me?" Max said with more force than he intended. "How long have you been back there?"

Drummond tilted his hat back. "I see. Fighting."

"Careful," Sandra said as she stared out the passenger window. "You don't want to poke your pale nose into this."

"Not trying to. But I assumed when you told me to be here this morning, it's because you needed me for something, right?"

"We're going to visit a witch — Madame Yan. I figured it was best if we all went."

"You're right about that, Doll. Silly for the two of you to go without some supernatural backup."

"My thoughts exactly. Nice to see I'm on the same wavelength as somebody in this group."

Max would have rolled his eyes, but he thought it best to pay attention to the road. Drummond went on, "What do we know about this Madame Yan?"

"Not much," Sandra admitted. "I found her on the Internet."

"What?" Max said. "I thought you knew her or had a recommendation."

"Oh, so now you want me to be a witch so I can provide a good recommendation."

"That's not what I meant."

"It's exactly what you meant." Sandra crossed her arms. "Make up your mind. Either it's too dangerous or you'll trust me to be able to handle it. But don't start wanting me to be a witch when it suits you."

Max started to speak, then thought better of it. At length, he asked Drummond, "You have any luck with your ghost?"

"I got it all set up for later. Don't worry."

"Gee, why would I ever worry?"

"Hey, you two want to have a fight, that's your business. Don't take it out on me."

Max took the ramp onto Route 8, made a left, and headed straight into Lexington. The sun was up, and the morning traffic had begun. They drove by a used car dealership lined with flags, an old factory with a FOR LEASE sign hanging in massive lettering, and a small building with the original name GUN SHOP painted on the side.

Max knew the area because of his forays into the wonders of Lexington barbecue. Like one of Pavlov's dogs, his mouth salivated at the thought of pulled-pork drenched in tangy, vinegar-based wonderfulness. He wanted to say that they should have set this meeting for lunchtime, but under the circumstances, he thought it best to keep quiet.

As they drove by Speedy's, a top quality barbecue joint, Sandra pointed to Rainbow Street. "Make a right here."

They turned up a narrow lane into a poorer section. All the homes were small with small yards — some with chain-link fencing, some with old trees, many littered with toys, bikes, or half-built cars.

Sandra pointed to a faded-yellow rancher. "That's the place." A station wagon that probably looked old in the 1980s sat in the drive. Max pulled up behind.

As they exited the car, Max noticed that the usual trappings of a witch's home were missing. No arcane symbols painted on the walkway or near the edge of the steps. No subtle yet ominous charms hanging on the porch — bone chimes or dreamcatchers or mojo bags. No line of salt across the lip of the front entranceway.

The front door stood ajar. A strange sign read: *Enter and wait.* Even stranger, Drummond had no trouble following them into the house.

They walked into a living room. Three couches pressed back against the walls. Paintings of old women from long ago hung above them. A hallway stretched off to the left. On the right side of the back wall, an arched opening led to the kitchen. From there, a woman approached.

She wore a black hijab over a white frock. Her smooth, olive skin and wrinkle-free dark eyes suggested she was in her early 20s. When she spoke, her strong North Carolinian accent jarred the image she had built up. "Welcome to Madame Yan's. I'm Cheryl-Lynn. Do you have an appointment?"

"We do," Sandra said. "Tell her the Porters are here."

Bowing slightly, Cheryl-Lynn backed her way into the kitchen. Max and Sandra held a look for a full two seconds before breaking into laughter. He covered his mouth and did his best to control the giggles, but they kept coming back. Sandra dropped to the couch and hid her face in the pillows.

Drummond said, "Will you two pull it together? She'll be back any second."

Max inhaled a deep breath, and despite a shaky exhale, he thought he had the laughter under control. Until he heard Sandra snort. The two fell into hysterics again.

Drummond scowled. "Oh, for Pete's sake. She's a Southern Muslim. What's the big deal? We got Korean Christians, too. Is that a thing to make you laugh?"

"We're sorry," Sandra said, dabbing at her eyes as she

regained her composure. "It took us by surprise. That's all."

Max inhaled deeply once more. "Yeah. I've seen plenty of Muslims around the area, but never heard one speak like that."

"How should they speak?" Drummond said. "They're just people like you and me."

"Don't get all high and mighty on us. Besides, how long did I have to work with you to stop you from calling black people *colored?*"

"I'm a product of my time. What's your excuse?"

Sandra stepped between them. "Boys, knock it off. You both know that neither one of you is a racist. So stop goading each other."

When Cheryl-Lynn returned, Max and Sandra had full control of themselves. They were respectful as they followed the young woman into the kitchen. At the cellar door, she turned back to them. "It's okay. You aren't the first to get a chuckle when I talk."

Sandra's face reddened. "We're sorry. We didn't mean to offend you."

"None taken."

"My husband and I have been under a lot of stress lately. Our laughter was more a release than anything else."

"It really is okay." Leaning closer with a faux-conspiratorial whisper, Cheryl-Lynn added, "Just don't start joking on Madame Yan. She's not likely to take it with kindness."

As they headed down the unfinished, wood stairs, Max offered a sheepish face, but Cheryl-Lynn either did not notice or did not care. Once they reached the basement, however, all such concerns vanished.

"Will you look at this place?" Drummond said.

The basement looked more like a medieval dungeon than an office or even a simple place for the laundry machine. Square-shaped, gray stones had been laid carefully to form the floor. In the center, a circular pool had been dug out. Clear water glistened with the light from four candles — one at each compass direction around the pool. A spell circle had been painted on the bottom of the pool.

Max glanced at Sandra but she shrugged — not a spell she knew yet.

Incense burned on a round table in the corner. The strong aroma masked the heavy chlorine smell rising from the pool. Animal heads decorated the walls, and from the worktable nestled underneath the staircase, Max surmised that either Madame Yan or Cheryl-Lynn had studied taxidermy.

"This way." Cheryl-Lynn led them toward the back. Another set of stairs had been dug into the floor. These stairs were cruder — not part of the original design to the house — and the walls pressed in tight on either side. A low ceiling forced Max to duck, and he had to hold the handrail or risk tumbling all the way down.

The temperature dropped. Max's skin prickled, and he sensed the weight of all that North Carolina red clay above his head. At the bottom, they entered a wide room with another low ceiling like a modern-day mine. Max half-expected a flat cart with miners flat on it would drive them the rest of the way.

Instead, Cheryl-Lynn pointed to a hanging bulb at the far end. "You'll find Madame Yan behind that door." She bowed and returned up the stairs.

As they scurried along the second basement, Drummond floated beside them. He had lowered his body into the floor so that his head would be on the same level as Max and Sandra without have to crouch. "I know I'm not the most advanced guy when it comes to the Internet, but how reliable is that machine for finding a useful witch?"

Sandra said, "The Internet isn't a machine. There isn't one building somewhere housing the Internet."

"You want to play *Parse Out Drummond's Question,* you go right ahead. I'm not the one bent over like a naughty schoolgirl waiting punishment."

Sandra stopped to look at him. "Have you been surfing Internet porn again?"

"Again?" Max said. "When did he do that before?"

"I caught him at it a few months ago."

Drummond said, "And you promised not to tell Max."

"I'm sorry, but you should know already that we can't keep a secret from each other for long. Look, I found Yan's listing on a witchcraft forum. There's no guarantee that she'll be good enough to help us, but we've got to start somewhere. Aren't you always telling us we need a network of contacts in the area? Well, we need witch contacts, too."

"I agree. I only question ..."

But Max did not hear the rest. His mind swirled around the idea of Drummond putting himself through the pain of touching the corporeal world so that he could use a mouse or type on a keyboard to find some porn. With a shudder, he drove out the images.

Drummond once had been a living man. He had his desires and weaknesses and flaws like any man. *I can't judge him for being human — well, for having been human once.* Besides, criticizing a person (or a ghost) for looking at porn was like criticizing a person for breathing — everybody did it to some extent.

They reached the door — an uneven, poorly hung thing made of five slats and painted blue. Orange light flickered around the edges. Max shivered. This all looked strange and unwelcoming to him; however, Sandra's calm, matter-of-fact approach eased his mind.

"Do you mind taking a look?" he asked Drummond.

"You know, you are entirely too comfortable using me like that. You ought to learn how to approach a suspicious door without me. What are you going to do if I ever move on and leave this ghostly world?"

"I don't see myself living hundreds of years until the Other forces you to move on, and since you've declined the opportunity in the past, I'm not too worried. Besides, isn't that part of why you stayed? To get in on all the detective action? Well, here you go."

Max did not miss the excited twinkle in Drummond's eyes. That ghost loved being a detective. "Okay," Drummond said. "I'll check it out for you. Wouldn't want Sandra getting hurt." The ghost stuck his head through the door. "It's okay. Just a big junk room, and an old lady poking about."

As Drummond floated back from the door, Max ducked around the bright, hanging bulb and knocked. Three sharp raps.

"Enter," a woman said in a sing-song voice as if entertaining guests at an evening soirée.

He pushed open the door, the bottom edge dug into the floor, and they slipped inside. The room had a normal ceiling, so Max and Sandra both stood straight and groaned as they stretched out cramped muscles. Despite the more open headroom, the furnishings cluttered up the place enough to feel even more claustrophobic than the narrow stairwell.

Madame Yan's place looked like a rummage sale gone amuck. Boxes of unknown contents had been stacked from floor to ceiling on one wall. Piles of books formed Jenga-like towers in front of the boxes. One corner had an assortment of empty birdcages. There was a mound of candlesticks next to a mound of half-used candles. One wall remained slightly clear due to a massive fireplace; however, long braids of hair had been hung from the ceiling, and many of them dangled dangerously close to the fire — the source of flickering light. Above the fireplace, a flatscreen had been mounted, and animal skulls formed a row along the mantelpiece.

Max leaned toward Sandra's ear and whispered, "Let's get this over with fast. It's a miracle this place hasn't burned to the ground."

Sandra nudged the edge of a throw rug (there were about twenty on the floor) to reveal the painted edges of a spell circle. "I don't think a miracle has anything to do with it."

"Ho!" the woman's voice sang out. "Madame Yan is here." An old lady appeared from a corridor masked by the numerous boxes sitting atop an old dresser. She wore a black-lace dress, and with an exuberant yet frazzled grin, Madame Yan walked to a high-backed chair and sat.

She had the most curious blend of heritage Max had ever seen. Her face bore features from all over the world — color, shape, and size lent itself from every continent. She was heavyset, yet when she moved, she flowed with uncommon grace.

"You must be Max and Sandra Porter," she said with an accent, clearly foreign yet imprecise as to what country she originated from. "What brings you here?"

Sandra stepped forward, but before she could speak, Drummond said, "Be careful. I'm feeling something strange here. More than a gut feeling, too."

"Thank you for seeing us on such short notice," Sandra said.

Madame Yan covered her mouth, hiding her smile. "Any time for you two."

"For us?" Max said. "What do you know about us?"

"Even if the two of you had not been responsible for the end of the Hull's reign over the witches here, I would know about you. Did you really think you could go around getting involved with witch covens and cursed paintings and the Baxter House and nobody else in our world would notice?"

"Hadn't really thought about it."

Drummond's hands went to his hips. "Hey, what about me? Why don't I get any credit?"

"Well, on behalf of all witches, we thank you. The Hulls had too much power for far too long. We all appreciate this opportunity you've provided." Madame Yan popped back on her feet. "Oh my, I'm being a terrible host. Would you like something to drink? I have bourbon and vodka, or if you'd prefer, I can ring down Cheryl-Lynn with some Irish coffee."

Max readied a comment concerning witches and alcohol, Sandra saved them both from his mouth. "No, thank you," she said. "It's a bit early in the morning for us."

With a shrug, Madame Yan returned to her chair. "If you say so. Living down here, I stopped seeing the point of day and night. There's only awake and asleep."

"You live down here? All the time?"

"I do. It's a long story and not interesting at all."

"I doubt that."

Madame Yan winked at Max. "Maybe you're right. Still, a witch's story is one of her many secrets, and we've only just met."

"Yet you already know a lot about us."

"Some days the advantage is yours. Today it belongs to me. Tomorrow, who knows?" Perhaps she spotted the frustration in his face because her voice rose in pitch as she made an expansive gesture. "You know how you should see me? Like one of those Tibetan monks. Cloistered away in the mountains so that they can meditate in peace. It's the same for me, except I'm hidden underground, that's all."

"Hidden from what?"

Sandra shot Max a hard look. "She doesn't want to talk about it."

Madame Yan tittered as if she had heard an amusing anecdote. "Being here has some advantages. A big one is that I've had time to read and read and read. I've learned from all the great books we have. And if it weren't for the pig-headed prejudices against witches, a lot of people in the world would benefit from these books." She stuck her hand between two boxes and pulled out a plate with two slices of cherry pie. A third slice had already been eaten. "Would either of you care for a nibble? Oh, probably not. Usually Cheryl-Lynn joins me for my meals. I forget myself sometimes." She set the plate aside. "You are obviously not here for a nibble. Are you? No, of course not. So, what is it that brings you to Madame Yan? Love potion, perhaps? Maybe a bit of divination? Or do you need my help with what's left of the Hulls?"

Despite her evasion, Max liked the sparkle in her eyes. "You're something."

"We all are something. Some of us are a bit more something than others."

Drummond chuckled. "You know, I might get to like this witch."

Stepping closer, Sandra said, "We've been involved in a case with two exhumed bodies, possibly exhumed by magic, and in each instance, the femur bone was stolen. I managed to see one of the bones, and it had symbols on it."

Madame Yan gestured to a stack of college notebooks. Two empty paint cans filled with pens and pencils sat on either side. Sandra took the top notebook and grabbed a pen. With a few swift strokes, she drew the symbols and handed the notebook over.

Pressing the notebook close to her face, Madame Yan inspected the work. "Are you sure these were the symbols?"

"Those are the ones I could memorize before losing the bone. There were more, though."

"I'm sure there were. This is only the first part of a dangerous spell."

Max edged in. "So, you know what it is?"

"Of course, I do. You don't get to be a witch as long as I have been and not be able to recognize a spell like that."

"Great. So, what is it?"

Madame Yan closed the notebook and tossed it on the floor. "You also don't get to be a witch as long as I have been and not know how this business works."

With a click of his tongue, Drummond said, "So much for liking her."

"You want payment? I thought you were so honored and appreciative of us getting rid of the Hulls."

She lifted her chin. "And I've thanked you for that. But this is business."

Sandra stepped forward again, her shoulder pushing Max back. "Please, ignore my husband. He's not good at dealing with our kind."

"Oh? You fancy yourself a witch?"

"I've only started learning. But maybe, a long time from now and after much learning, maybe if I'm lucky, I can rise to a status as high as yours." Max tensed, but Sandra showed no sign of noticing. She went on, "I suppose I'll have to go fumble around for a bit to figure out those symbols, or maybe they're easy to find. You seemed to know them quite fast. I'm sure I just need to look in a few more books. Besides, if I don't succeed, I can always find another witch to help me."

Madame Yan shifted in her chair as she filled with pride. "Well, perhaps to help a novice get started on the right track, I might be able to provide a little information. After all, so many so-called witches out there would steer you wrong."

Sandra gave a slight bow. "Thank you. We do appreciate your efforts."

"Nonsense. We witches have to look out for each other."

Drummond clapped his hands together in a sharp, single strike. "Doll, you're one of the best. That's as serious a case of buttering up as I've ever seen. Straight to the point, not overdone, but hitting all the right notes."

Though torn between a desire to wrest Sandra from the lure of witchcraft and a desire to hug her for her strength of will, Max merely stood silent. Drummond saw it as skilled manipulation, but Max knew her determination drove her diplomacy and ultimately, her success. She never ceased to amaze him.

Madame Yan planted her hands on her knees and squinted at them. "Now, let me tell you about this spell."

Chapter 12

"IT IS THE CALL TO POWER," Madame Yan said. Though her eyes repeatedly shifted between Max to Sandra, Max noticed that she lingered her gaze longer upon his wife. "It's not a controversial spell by far, but in my opinion, it should be. It's difficult to cast, but in the wrong hands, the Call to Power can be a devastating spell."

"What does it do?" Max asked.

Madame Yan bristled at his impatience. To Sandra, she said, "On a basic level, the spell is used to lock in magic energy for later use. You can put the energy into almost anything."

"Even bone?" Max asked.

"Yes, most often bone. Now, please, stop interrupting me."

"I was just asking a question."

Though Sandra's face remained impassive, her voice snapped out with force. "Max, show her some respect."

Drummond looked like he wanted to chime in with some sarcasm, but a quick glance from Sandra stopped him. To Madame Yan, Sandra said, "Please, continue."

"The storage of energy could be used for anything. Long ago, witches would use it so they could access large amounts of energy quickly in times of battle. More often, though, witches would invoke the Call to Power as they neared death. They would carve their own bones before dying, and infuse the bones with all the energy they had. They passed their power down to the next generation, and in this way, the family line would continue no matter what happened. After all, not every daughter is touched with the gift. With this spell, even the most mundane girl could potentially become a powerful witch."

She scooted to the side of her chair and reached for the notebook. Looking over the symbols again, Madame Yan tapped the page. "These are an older variation of the spell. Not common at all. Probably not found in many books, but there aren't many spells that use all three of those symbols together. Whoever did this is either quite esoteric or she cast the spell quite a long time ago."

Max said, "We suspect it's the latter."

"Then you should be extra careful. The older witches spent their lives fighting prejudice unlike anything we have in the modern world. We feel we are oppressed, and we still are, but at the same time, we have greater rights and recognition than ever in the history of our people. An older witch, one attempting to pass her power down through generations, is going to be the kind that felt the harsh hand of those prejudices. She will have seen her peers run out of their homes, thrown in the lake with stones tied to their legs, and of course, burned at the stake. She will be the kind of mean-spirited hag that populated children's stories."

Sandra's face darkened. "And that's the kind of energy she'll have passed along."

"Yes, yes. You see. That's good. You're smart. Evil begets evil with this spell. That's what makes it so dangerous."

Max's stomach soured. "Our enemy has two of these bones."

"Ah," Madame Yan said. "Then you must destroy the third before your enemy gets hold of it."

"There's a third?"

Drummond sighed. "There is always a third."

Madame Yan got to her feet and crossed over to her bottle of vodka. After pouring a tumbler, she said, "The number three contains great power. Many things in the universe revolve around the concept of three. For the Call to Power, the witch's energy is imbued into three of the same object — in your case, human bones — and only with all three bones can a person tap into the magic stored within."

"Our enemy is a man. Will it work for him, or must it be a woman from a witch line?"

Madame Yan winked at Sandra. "He doesn't listen too well,

does he?" To Max, she said, "Magic is magic. Witches may have developed this spell to secure their power, but anybody who has the three bones and knows what they are doing can gain the power."

More to himself than to anybody else in the room, Max muttered, "Then we've got to find Edward Wallace quick."

Madame Yan slammed down her vodka. "Wallace?"

"You know the name?"

"Oh, yes, I most certainly do." She shuffled back to her chair like a Romero zombie, clumsily knocking over a stack of books in the process. "Abagail Wallace is a name that all Southern witches learn about."

"Abagail," Max whispered — the name that Leon Moore had mentioned.

"She was the type of witch that reveled in our darker side, that made life harder for those of us trying to be good people. That's the thing most people out in the world fail to understand — the majority of witches are normal, everyday people who only want good for their lives and those around them. Their views may not be the same as yours but they aren't crazy or ignorant or malicious or racist or any other tag you want to attach. But some witches, those on the fringe of our people, they are the ones spouting nonsense and acting horribly. They are the ones that make a bad name for the rest of us. Oh, I have no doubt we are talking about the same Wallace name. Like the Hulls, she was obsessed with building power. This spell would be something she would have undoubtedly used. And that's terrible. She was terrible. So bad that many myths built up around the things she did and quickly became the stories told to witch children to scare them into behaving well."

Max knew trouble when he heard it — and anybody frightening enough to scare witches meant a lot of trouble. Though part of him loathed asking, he had to know what they faced. "What stories?"

"Horrible tales. She would lure witches deep into the backcountry, promising to teach them her secret rituals. They would go through the motions of a grand spell, or so she told them, and it always involved drinking some concoction. She drugged them this way. Then she would string them up by the ankles and cut them apart like deer. That would be enough to scare any child from wandering too deep into the woods, but it didn't end there. See, the witch coven at the time formed the equivalent of a posse and went after her. Thirteen witches in all, and only one returned. She had lost an arm and her mind. But from her ramblings, we know that Abagail Wallace cooked and consumed the other witches."

"Yeah," Max said. "That would probably scare a kid or two."

"And that was one of the tamer stories." She rubbed her chin. "This must be the same Wallace. A Wallace always pops up in times of weakness. With no ruling party at the moment, it makes sense that one would show up now."

Sandra asked, "If we don't find the third bone, what then? Is there a spell that will stop the Call to Power?"

"No," Madame Yan said. "It's time for you to leave. Go find that bone. Good luck."

As if a machine had been turned off, she rested her head against the back of her chair and closed her eyes. Max and Sandra waited until they realized that was it. The witch would not move again until they left.

"Time to go," Drummond said. "We won't get anything else here."

They wound their way back across the low-ceiling stretch and up to the main basement. Cheryl-Lynn met them there and escorted them upstairs and out of the house. With a cheery wave, she said, "Thanks for coming by. See y'all next time."

Walking to the car, Max said, "Looks like we've got to find that bone. Any ideas where to start?"

Drummond said, "You two sit tight. I'll go get my ghost. He'll have something worth saying. I'm sure of it. Then we can figure it out from there."

"Sounds good to me. I got nothing else, anyway."

After Drummond left, Max held the car door for his wife. She had a dark frown as she sat. "What's wrong?"

"I can't figure out why Madame Yan lied to us."

Chapter 13

THEY DROVE BACK ON ROUTE 8, a little further down, and parked in a strip mall next to a McDonald's. Max turned the car off and shifted in his seat to face Sandra. "What did she lie about?"

"When I asked her if there was a spell to break the Call to Power in case we don't get the bone, she said there wasn't one."

"So?"

"She lied. I could see it on her face, for one. But the fact is that all spells have an opposite. It's like a balanced scale. There's a spell that creates light, so there's one that creates dark. If there's a spell to open a door, there's one to close it. Always. It's the first thing I learned when I started studying witchcraft. It's foundational."

"Guess she didn't realize how much you already know."

"You're not listening close enough. *It's the first thing I learned* — literally, the first. There's no way she could think I didn't know that would be a lie."

"So, either she's a loon that's completely incompetent — which is not impossible — or she purposely said this to get you to do the opposite." Max did not sound convinced. "If she wanted you to find a spell like that, why not hand you the right book and point to it? Or if she didn't have the spell on hand or didn't know it, why not at least tell you where to look?"

Sandra's eyes widened. "She couldn't because she was afraid."

"Of what?"

"No. Of who."

Max shared Sandra's stunned expression. "Mother Hope."

"I think so. Look at it — Madame Yan told us everything we asked but the most important part. At the same time, she didn't really tell us much. We got specific details, but nothing we wouldn't have found out in the long run."

"Maybe. It's hard to say. Whatever her reasons, though, she definitely drew the line at helping us find that spell." Max squirmed in his seat. "You really think Mother Hope was listening in on us?"

"I think Madame Yan thought it was possible. The only other time I've seen a witch act that nervously was with the Hulls, and they are not worth getting worked up about anymore."

Max shifted back in his seat and scanned the parking lot as he thought. Sandra did the same. As he listened to the cars shush by and smelled the seductive aroma of hamburgers, he put his right hand on the spot between them, palm up, and waited. He pushed all thoughts out of his head, content to observe the people walking in and out of the Food Lion grocery.

Her hand laced in his.

He clenched her fingers but said nothing. Though not the full end of their earlier argument, not even half-of-a-reconciliation, this simple gesture brought them a step closer. More importantly, it allowed them to continue working the case without having to tiptoe around each other. The rest of the argument had been postponed, and he could feel the relief in the air.

Seven minutes later, Drummond appeared on the right side of the backseat. He gestured to the empty space on the left side. "Max, Sandra, I'd like you to meet Chester Stanton. Chester, these are the two I told you about. Now, only the lady can see you, but Max here's dealt with ghosts before. Even though he can't see or hear you, he'll get enough translation from me and the lady."

Max twisted around the seat to look back at the empty space. "Nice to meet you Mr. Stanton. If you don't mind, I'm going to have my wife tell me what she sees. It'll help me a bit if I can visualize what you look like. That okay?"

Sandra nodded. "He says it's fine. Chester is thin and a bit shorter than Drummond. He's wearing an outfit that I think is from the right time period — kind of a brownish cloth with a leather satchel on his side. He's got a tricorn hat and knee-high, black boots. He says he was born in 1748. Dark hair, bit of stubble, and a large nose. Sorry, Mr. Stanton, but it's true."

"Hey," Drummond said, "you've been dead for over two hundred years. I don't think vanity is really a worthwhile trait to bother with anymore."

Max cleared his throat. "Has Mr. Drummond explained to you why we wanted to talk?"

"Of course, I did."

"Come on, let the man talk for himself."

It amazed Max how easily he and Drummond played off each other now. Without any previous plan, Drummond had set Max up to be the good guy. It wasn't exactly a good cop/bad cop play, but it had the effect of raising Max's status in the eyes of the interviewee.

For that same reason, Max turned to Sandra for the translation. She said, "He knows we've been looking into the Regulators."

"That's right," Max said. He tried to picture where Stanton's eyes should be and put his focus on that spot. "There were three men that we are investigating. The only name we know anything about is Archibald Henderson. Did you know him?"

Speaking for Stanton, Sandra said, "'No, I did not, but I was there at the Battle of Alamance, and I know much about what transpired.'"

"What about Johnathan Shoemaker?"

"'I don't know him. I'm trying to tell you about Alamance.'"

Drummond said, "First, tell them why you're going to be so helpful."

"'Your associate here has explained that you are aware of the Other and the lives we lead in this ghostly realm. I have been here for a long time. I've watched as one friend after another moved on to the afterlife we all seek. I tried for decades to let go of whatever held me to this Earth, but to no avail. I fear that I may forever be bound in this undead form.'"

Max opened his mouth, intent on explaining that eventually all ghosts move on, but Drummond put up his hand. "Go on, Stanton. They need to hear this so they get why this is so important to you."

"'I finally realized that the only souls to move on are the ones that atoned for their sins. I cannot apologize to or ask forgiveness from those I have wronged. They are gone. I am all that's left. It is maddeningly lonely.'"

Drummond looked away and pursed his lips. Max glanced over but caught Sandra's warning look — whatever Drummond's thoughts, he clearly wanted to keep them to himself. If he wanted complete privacy, he could disappear into the Other. Still, Max and Sandra did their best to keep the focus on Stanton.

"So," Max said, "you've decided to talk with us because you're lonely?"

"'You misjudge me. I am not some vagrant looking for solace from your companionship. Rather, I seek to council you on what I know in the service of appeasing the Lord and being lifted away from this dreadful existence. I wish to move on, and if providing this information is of use to you, I am happy to do so, should it aid my cause.'"

Drummond flipped his hands open like a magician. "There you have it. You ask me for a source, and here he is. So, Stanton, now you can tell us about this battle you were in."

Sandra leaned toward Max. "He's taking a moment to compose himself. He looks a bit shaken as he's thinking about it all."

"Take your time," Max said to Stanton.

When the ghost was ready, Sandra signaled Max and returned to the job of translating. "'The situation had been brewing for years. Tryon for the Crown and Husband for the people. Those two men clashed over and over, but always and without fail, they did so in the civil battlefield of politics.'"

"Didn't Husband orchestrate riots?"

"'I would hardly characterize them as riots, but I will grant you that politics can become a more physical endeavor from time to time. However, when we congregated in the wooded rise in Alamance, we expected nothing more than the opportunity for a peaceful protest. We were going to declare our grievances and attempt, once more, to reform the corrupt system we lived under.'"

Stanton grew quiet, but based on the reactions of Drummond and Sandra, Max did not press. It appeared that Stanton had been overcome by the memory.

At length, Sandra continued for Stanton, "'I remember watching those bastards arrive. They marched in their straight lines and smart dress. Their feet hit the ground in unison. It was a horrendous sound, and I would be lying if I did not admit that the ferocious noise intimidated me. They lined up at the far end of the field that lay between the two edges of woods — hundreds of men. And the cannons. They wheeled them out one after the other. Twenty, maybe thirty of them.

"'I suppose we should have recognized that this time would be different, that Tryon not only displayed his strength, but in doing so, in bringing such weaponry to the field, he declared to us that he tired of dealing with the Regulators and would see it finished that day. We sent a few men to parlay with Tryon, this was customary back then — I do not recall how many men nor how many times they conversed, but I do know they went out more than once.

"'And then, without warning — at least, without a warning we understood to be serious — they opened fire upon us. Or perhaps we shot first. I imagine the history that has been documented knows better. For my part, I stood in a crowd of men discussing, or more accurately complaining, about the situation when suddenly we heard muskets snapping off and then a cannon blast.

"'The battle, well, I do not think you could call it that for long. The cannons were dangerous but had a short range. A few of our bravest men fought back, taking positions behind trees or wherever possible. A narrow gully ran between the forces and one of our men, James Pugh, lodged himself at the foot of a large boulder in the gully. The cannons ripped apart the landscape near him, but he held on, taking shots at the enemy. We cheered him and rallied others to fight on. But we had not come to fight, and while many of us did bear arms, many more had left their weapons at home so as not to provoke a violent reaction."'

Drummond said, "I guess that didn't pan out so well."

"'No. Tryon's men overpowered us. We broke apart, many of us taking refuge in the surrounding woods. While most of us were able to melt back into our towns and farms, Tryon needed to make an example of somebody. He rounded up those whom he could identify without doubt as traitors to the Crown, and he had them executed. Six men hanged for what had occurred at Alamance."'

Max pointed. "And you were one of those six?"

"'Not at all. I managed to free myself of any connection to the incident. I rented a small dwelling from the Moravians near the city of Winston, and I expected to live my remaining days there. But that was not to be. A terrible night came to me about two years later.

"'I do not know what spirituality you hold, but I will tell you that in my life, I have known those who are capable of dark things, of spellcraft and brews. Though I cannot prove this to be the case, it is my sincerest belief that Governor Tryon hired these women of darkness to exact revenge upon those of us he wanted to hurt but could not do so within the bounds of law."'

"Wait," Max said. "Are you saying that Tryon hired a witch to curse you?"

"'Indeed, he did. I share this with you because your associate suggested that you might be able to help me move on. Not only in the telling of my tale, but that you might be persuaded to seek out my remains and lift my curse."'

Max looked to Drummond, but the ghost made a slight shrug and said nothing. To Stanton, Max said, "Do you know where your body rests?"

"'Rest, it does not. I have not rested in centuries, but yes, I do know the location of my remains. And I will give you that information provided that when you find them, you will set me free."'

"We'll try. I can't promise anything more than that. We will try our best."

"Wait," Drummond said and reached across the seat.

Sandra slumped. "He's gone."

"But he didn't tell us where to go. I can try to find him in the Other. I'll make him tell us."

Max's phone chimed. Not a phone call but a text. Who would bother to text him other than Sandra? He unlocked his phone and found a simple message: *Twin City Stage, Coliseum Drive, W-S*

"That's a first," Max said. "Text by ghost."

Chapter 14

AFTER DROPPING SANDRA OFF at the office so she could research spell books and online forums in an effort to find a counter to the Call to Power, Max and Drummond drove to the Twin City Stage. Located on the northern side near Wake Forest University, the theater had been around since 1935 and had earned a reputation as one of the cultural necessities of the city. But why would Chester Stanton have been buried there?

No. I've got a more important problem to deal with first.

He pulled the car over to the shoulder. To Drummond's questioning eyes, Max said, "Would you please give me a few minutes of privacy? I've got to make a call."

"Now? We've got to get ourselves ready to find that body."

"I'm calling my mother."

Drummond's face slackened. "Oh." He pulled up the lapels of his coat collar. "Five minutes enough?"

"More than enough."

"Good luck," he said and disappeared.

Max brought out his phone and rang his mother. When she answered, he told her the truth — that his case had become more complicated and that he had to cancel their lunch. He promised to take her out to dinner that night, something nice, just the two of them, but he could feel the ice coming through the phone.

"No need," she said in a near-monotone. "I shouldn't have expected you to change your schedule for me. I'm just your mother, and one thing all mothers learn is that we are always taken for granted."

"It's not like that."

"Why should we expect different? After all, we're always there when you need us. No matter what you do, there we are."

"Please, listen to me. This case is important."

"Of course, of course. Work is always important. A mother understands."

"I will take you out. I promise. But it can't be this afternoon. That's all."

"I'll make sure to eat a snack beforehand, just in case."

Max cringed at the hurt in her voice and the pleading in his. He knew he was wrong, and she knew how to milk that guilt. But more than that old pattern playing out yet again between them, Max thought about her evening talks with J and about the loss of her friend. He wanted to tell her that she could stay with him or that he would set her up in a nice apartment or a condo or anything they could find around the city. She would be close to family, and she could trust that he would be there for her. But why would she believe him when he couldn't even keep a simple lunch date?

He apologized several more times until his mother became silent. With a meek assurance that he would see her later that night for dinner, he finished the call.

When Drummond returned and looked at Max, he clicked his tongue. "I take it things didn't go too well."

"Don't worry about it," Max said, started the car, and pulled back into traffic.

"If you need me to, I can go tell Sandra you want to talk. I realize she's not the most sympathetic ear when it comes to your mother, but it's better than nothing."

"Forget about it, please."

Propping his feet on — well, through — the dashboard, Drummond said, "Consider it forgotten. Let's focus on Chester Stanton."

"Gladly. I don't trust him."

"We're in agreement there. I've got to say I'm impressed. I didn't like the way he looked — always fidgeting with his hands and whenever he answered a question from you, he'd look around like the answer was written on the upholstery or something. But you couldn't see him. What makes you not trust him?"

Before answering, Max replayed the conversation in his head. "For starters, he claims to be buried in a theater that wasn't built until around 150 years after he died. And while he promises us he was with the Regulators, that he was at the actual Battle of Alamance, the details are inaccurate."

"I don't want defend the guy, but it has been a long time. Maybe he's fuzzy but that doesn't make him a liar."

"Then there was his whole thing about witches. Why bring that up? Most people, dead or alive, would be hesitant to talk about witches and magic. You don't know if the other party is going to take it well or have you committed. But Stanton just breaks into song about it as if he already knew we were well-acquainted with witches."

Drummond tapped his pursed lips. "That is strange. It's true that we're developing a good reputation of being the people to deal with the unusual cases, and it's possible Stanton concluded that if you're okay dealing with ghosts, then you probably deal with witches, too, but he didn't strike me as the kind that would keep up on such things. He's more of the *keep my head buried until I move on* kind of ghost."

"Something's off in what he told us. And I don't even want to think about how he texted my cellphone."

Max turned up a steeped driveway that led to a parking lot on the side of the building. All brick like a high school but about a tenth of the size. Old trees drooped over the walkway. Like so much of Winston-Salem, and North Carolina in general, many of the buildings mixed the old and new. The trees mixed with the brick building. A wall-length series of windows mixed with a heavily locked door.

But the locks had been broken.

"You see that?" Max said.

"I guess I should go in ahead and check for any danger to you."

"Of course there's danger to me. That broken lock means Edward Wallace is here. Last time, he beat me pretty bad. Still hurts. He's after that bone, now, and we've got to stop him. So, yes, there's plenty of danger."

With a stern, pointed finger, Drummond said, "I'm going to chalk up your snide attitude to the fact that you had to deal with your mother. Otherwise, I can leave, and you can face Mr. Call to Power all by yourself."

"Okay. You've made your point. Would you kindly look in the lobby to see if I'm about to get jumped when I go in there?"

"Sure. No problem." Drummond stepped through the wall and returned. "All clear in there. You want me to check the whole place?"

"Yes, but let's take a step at a time. I'd like to have you at my side as much as possible."

This frank admission appeared to work on Drummond. He lowered his hat and narrowed his eyes. "Good thinking. We should always be there to back up a partner."

Max opened the door and entered a wide, oddly-shaped lobby. The long wall of windows shed afternoon light across the dark interior. Thin carpeting covered the floor and the walls had large photo displays of past performances — mostly musicals and comedies plus a few sparse dramas. A hall stretched off to the right, presumably toward offices. The back wall formed an L with the main doors to the theater at the corner. Stairs climbed up to the theaters door on the right while a long ramp for wheelchair access followed the long-side of the wall.

Max peered down the hall but it was too dark to make anything out. He saw a door with an opening for tickets and decided to check it out first. "You ever get lonely?"

"What?" Drummond said, pulling his head back from a closet door.

"I was thinking how you've been around for a long time. Decades past what the majority from your era would live through. You must get lonely."

"This about your mother?"

"All her friends have died off."

Drummond floated over, taking off his hat and holding it by the rim. "Look, we all want to be understood, and that means having people you can relate to, people who understand you. It's hard when every reference you make is met with a confused look. It's even harder when everything around you no longer makes sense. Tweets and posts and emojis and data plans and countless other words that back in the day would make no sense or have vastly different meanings. It's like waking up in a foreign country."

"But you seem okay with us. I mean Sandra and I are your contacts into the world, and I don't see you going batty because of it."

"Doesn't mean I wouldn't love to hang out with a gal from my era, talk about all the crazy things we did to survive during the Depression, reminisce, that kind of thing."

Max walked up the ramp and stopped at the theater doors. "Do I need to ask?"

"We're back to that? In that case, yes, you do need to ask. It would show a little respect."

Biting back a laugh, Max nodded. "Will you please check ahead for me?"

"Happy to do it."

For the few seconds after Drummond slid through the wall, Max held on to the levity of their bickering. It helped fight back the tension crawling underneath his skin. Walking through an empty, dark building that he expected to find something bad inside never got easier — even during daylight. But Max appreciated some sharp banter, a snide joke, or anything that relieved his mounting nerves. He suspected Drummond felt the same.

"I can't see anything, but there ain't much light," Drummond said when he returned.

Max pulled open the door and stepped inside. He could feel the slope of the auditorium, and he could see the stage in the distance. The large room stood in darkness except for a lone, bare bulb atop a stand. The stand had been placed in the center of the stage. It cast a pale light that formed hundreds of strange shadows stretching off in all directions.

"You know what that's called?" Drummond said with a

snicker. "They call it a *ghost lamp*."

As Max crept toward the stage, passing row upon row of seats that he could barely see, he tried to focus on anything but the idea that something would jump him at any moment. "Ghost lamp? How do you know that?"

"You serious? The theater was still a big thing in my time."

"I can't see much back here, but I don't think there's a coffin to be found."

"Yeah." Drummond lowered his head with a slight shake. "I don't like that. I suppose this means I've got to go down there."

"Down where?"

"Underground. Way I see this, either Chester Stanton lied to us or his body is somewhere underground. I don't like going down there. You think this is dark, try being six feet under where no light comes through. You can feel that cold nothing pressing in on you. Only reason I can see anything down there is that I'm dead. Gives me a little edge."

"How long will that take?"

"It's a big area. Five, maybe ten minutes. Maybe more."

"Then I'll check out the stage and any other side rooms I find."

Drummond nodded. "Be careful of the pit."

"The pit?"

"Orchestra pit. The section right in front of the stage where the musicians play. This theater has a pit that drops down to a room beneath. I'll check that out before I go underground."

Max's eyes had adjusted as much as they were going to, and he still had trouble seeing. However, he could make out the edge of the stage and a set of portable steps placed in front of a small wall. The steps were a few feet from the stage and a wooden plank bridged them together. Beneath was darkness — the orchestra pit.

"I see it," Max said. "I'll be fine. But hurry, please. If Stanton lied, then we've been sent out here to keep us from wherever we should be."

"That's what bothers me." Without further comment, Drummond lowered through the floor, leaving Max with his foot on the first step.

He reached out as if to stop Drummond but pulled his hand back. He needed his partner to check for the coffin underground. No way around that — even if it meant being stuck alone in an empty, dark chamber lit only by a ghost lamp.

He waited but when Drummond did not return, he realized it would be a long time before the ghost could check every square foot of space. Drummond would have to also check the ground beneath the parking lot and the surrounding area. A coffin buried two-hundred-plus years ago could be anywhere on the property.

Max climbed the steps and walked out on the board. He made sure to keep his eyes looking ahead and not once did he peek beneath. Not that he expected to see anything — the pit would be a pool of darkness — but he feared losing his balance in all the empty space.

Once safely on the stage, he moved quickly forward. The light from the ghost lamp did not reach out as far as Max had hoped, and he found himself wishing he had brought a flashlight. He could go back to the car and grab one. Except that would require navigating his way back up the dark theater. Without Drummond, he would move slow and cautious, and in the end, he would waste more time than he wanted to give to this place.

As he walked the stage, he checked the wings. Nobody there. No coffin, either. Just some chairs, various props laid out on a table, large coils of rope, a few paint cans, and two dresses hung next to a black curtain.

He heard a noise like a pebble dropped on the floor. Moving slowly, Max stepped out from the wings. He didn't see anybody, and he couldn't tell where the sound had come from.

He opened his mouth. *No. Don't alert anybody.* He inched toward the edge of the stage, peering down into the darkness. His shadow, created by the ghost lamp, stretched across the stage and fell into the pit.

I'm so dumb. I've got a bare bulb behind me illuminating the entire stage. Why should I worry about calling out? Who's going to be suddenly alerted to my presence when all anybody has to do is look at the stage? Here I am. A laugh grew in his chest, and he struggled to hold it back.

"Hey, Max." Edward Wallace called out.

Max jumped as he spun his head back toward the ghost lamp. A large shadow loomed over him. He had time to wonder how Edward planned to handle the moment. That wondering did not last long. Edward's lips rose into a satisfied smile as he thrust a fist into Max's gut. Then, as Max bent over, he threw an uppercut and sent Max flailing backward toward the pit.

Chapter 15

AGAINST THE DARK BACKDROP of the ceiling, Max saw stars. Lots of them. Little sparkles and swirls. His hand dangled over the chasm of the orchestra pit and his stomach throbbed where he had been struck.

Edward's black shoes gently clicked against the wood stage, then the wood plank, and finally stopped on the top of the movable stairs. He squatted so that Max could see him, albeit upside-down.

With his elbows resting on his knees, Edward said, "Sorry about that, but I didn't think you'd listen to me otherwise."

"Oh, sure." Max groaned as he sat up. "This is the perfect way to get me to listen. I really care about what you want to say now."

Edward brushed his pants. With a self-deprecating laugh, he walked back to the stage. "I admit that I can be too forceful at times. It's part of the baggage that comes with my family. We've been held back so often in our lives, had to struggle for each step forward, that we often see a fight when none exists. Still, if you'll be honest, I don't think you would have sat and talked with me had I simply greeted you."

"Probably not." Max started to stand, but Edward put out his hand. Max curled his lips. "I see. The forceful bit isn't over yet."

"That's up to you."

Max doubted that. Guys like Edward Wallace acted more like politicians — saying one thing while visibly doing another. He would stop being forceful only when it suited him. Apparently, that would be after he said whatever he wanted to say.

Max's eyes widened. "This was all a set up. There's no

skeleton here. Was Chester Stanton even with the Regulators?"

"I don't talk with the dead, so I can't help you there. That part was arranged by my ancient grandmother, Abagail. But yes, there is no skeleton here. Not that it would matter. I already have all three bones. You can't stop what is coming."

Max leaned over on his elbow. It relieved some of the pain radiating from his stomach, but doing so also opened his legs up. Now, all he had to do was wait for an opportunity.

"Wait," he said, making a bigger show of thinking. "You said you don't talk with the dead. Isn't Abagail dead? I mean when you say she's ancient, we're talking about a couple centuries."

Despite the pale ghost lamp, Edward's eyes shined. "Abagail Wallace birthed this family line and gave us the strength and gifts to build something of greatness. Not all of us speak with the dead, but some always do. Those individuals are our conduit to dear Abagail."

Max smacked his forehead. "Oh, man, you guys are trying to resurrect her. Look, I've been through this before with the Hulls. Trust me. It's not a good idea."

"The Hulls are charlatans compared to Abagail. And no, we are not trying to resurrect her. She is content in the Other and strong enough to resist moving on. At least, she resists until I have fulfilled our family's destiny to rule the magic community here."

"You want to be the next Hulls?"

"Tucker Hull and his cronies stole our rightful position. The 1700s were not the most enlightened time for women, and Hull used that to his advantage. He knew Abagail was stronger and a more capable leader of witches, but he wanted it for himself. Women had a low-enough standing that he hardly had to work to take over." Edward stepped closer — but not close enough. "The Wallace family should have been the ones to run things around here, and now we will."

"Right." Max tried to scoot towards Edward but too much motion would be noticeable. "That's what the bones are for. You plan to take over using Abagail's power stored in those bones."

Edward's eyebrows rose. "I guess it's true about your little firm. You really are good at research."

"It wasn't that hard to find out about the Call to Power, which is why I can tell you that you're not going to succeed. It won't be any harder to find a way to stop your spell. And the Magi —"

"The Magi." Disdain punctuated each syllable as he stepped even closer. "Mother Hope is more a criminal than any of us and far more of a threat. But she is no match for Abagail."

Still too far off. But if Max could provoke one more advance, Edward might be in range.

"That's it, huh? You're just another one of the power-hungry. You'll do anything to gain control over other people."

"Don't act like you're superior. You're doing the same thing."

"I am?"

"Of course. Mother Hope wants to control the power around here. So do I. You lend your strengths to one side or the other, and in doing so, you exert your control over the outcome. Wasn't it you who took down the Hulls? You decided they shouldn't have power, and you made that a reality."

"That's different."

"Why? Because you didn't feel greedy, perhaps? That's a lie. Everybody is greedy for something. And think for a moment what our lives will be like if I am not the winner in all of this. If Mother Hope wins out, the Magi will come down hard on all the witches. Either you will belong to their select group and benefit from it, or you'll have to go into hiding, practice your craft in secret, and pray that she never discovers you. She's not above torture."

Max winced. "I'm aware of that."

"Maybe Mother Hope and I both fail to take over. Then you have anarchy. Witches doing whatever they want to whomever they want. It wouldn't be long until the rest of the world took notice. They probably still wouldn't believe in witchcraft, but they would see a troubled city and the state police, maybe even the US military, would be called in to quell the unrest."

"You paint a pretty grim picture. I suppose we'll have unicorns and rainbows under your lead."

Edward smiled and the stage brightened. The man had the most charming face. But Max could see the razor teeth beneath the mask.

"If I gain power, I don't promise some sort of utopia. I do think that I will keep the world stable. I won't use the witches for my personal vengeance like the Hulls did nor would I abuse them like Mother Hope would most certainly do. I will do the job of any good leader. I will keep the ship steering clear and true. I will let the witches do as they please so long as they do not jeopardize our stability. That's it. And it truly is that simple."

"Wow. You almost sound reasonable."

"What I want," Edward said, moving two steps closer, "is to offer you a job."

Max had been ready to strike, but this threw him. "What?"

"Help me succeed, and I'll hire you. Not as a researcher, but as an advisor. I want you to be the one to make sure I do not cross those lines that lead to corruption. I want you to help me avoid becoming another Hull or a Mother Hope."

Max had to admit that sounded smart. And reasonable. And well considered. Perhaps his family had spent the last several generations preparing for this moment, weighing the good and the bad of all those that came before, setting and resetting their course until finally they had someone like Edward. They taught him how to lead, how to keep balance, how to fight greed and corruption.

Then again, Edward was a manipulative bastard who attacked Max and Sandra at the bog, showing no interest in balance or peace or anything good.

"Nice proposal," Max said. "Too bad you're full of crap."

He swept his left leg in a wide arc and connected with Edward's calf. The young man yelped in surprise as he tumbled, slamming his side into the stage.

No time to stand. Max scuttled across the few feet between

them and moved right atop the young man's chest. Pressing his elbow into Edward's sternum, Max made a tight fist with his free hand and punched. He pulled back and punched again. Both blows landed on the jaw.

Edward's head lolled to the side. Max flexed his hand — hitting bone hurt. All of his fingers still moved, though, so he probably had not broken any bones of his own.

As he pondered the durability of his hand, Edward rocked to the left, tossing Max to the floor. Max tried to roll away, but he had lost sense of his position on the stage. If he made a mistake, he could roll right into the orchestra pit. That hesitation proved to be a mistake as well.

Edward had managed to stand. Like a furious beast determined to open up its prey, he kicked and punched and tore at Max's side. The previous bruises could not numb the pain.

Max screamed. Tears drenched his face. Each strike shivered bolts of fire along his skin. Jagged waves of pain. He curled into a fetal ball, offered no resistance, but still the attack continued. He tried to protect his ribs with his arms, but the blows shifted towards his back.

"I will run this city," Edward yelled as he pummeled Max.

"Yes, yes. You win." Max would have said anything to stop the beating.

Edward reached down and grabbed a chunk of Max's shirt. With a strong grunt, he yanked Max into a seated position. Max stared at this twisted face — both handsome and terrifying.

Stepping back and breathing hard, Edward pointed at Max like a scolding parent. "You shouldn't do that sort of thing. I don't like to see such disrespect from my employees." Max must have had an incredulous look on his face, but he could hardly feel anything beyond a constant ache. Edward put his hands on his hips. "Okay, one more time. I offer you a job working for me. Last chance to do the right thing here. Any other decision is going to bring you more pain, and I've got to say that you don't look like you can take anymore."

Max raised his head and grinned. "You know how you've

got Abagail working for you from the Other?"

"Yeah?"

"You're not the only one with a friend in the Other."

Edward frowned as he pieced it together. Realization widened his expression as he whirled around. Before he stopped turning, Drummond cracked him across the head and dropped him to the ground. Two more sharp jabs knocked Edward unconscious.

"Ready to go?" Drummond said, but to Max the words sounded garbled and distant.

His head swirled. He felt his lips tremble upward as part of him knew that Edward had been stopped, but the rest of him drifted backwards. Only a sliver of his mind noted that he sat near the orchestra pit — man, he hated that pit. The rest of him kept thinking how wonderful it would feel to lay his head on a soft pillow, close his eyes, and sleep for a few days.

The ice that gripped his wrist shot frozen bullets through his blood. His eyes snapped open. Everything was lopsided shadows and pale ghost light. And a ghost, too — Drummond.

"Come on, Max! Wake up!"

In the next second, Max's brain put the pieces together. He had fallen back into the pit, his ankles caught on the ledge, and Drummond had halted his fall by grabbing his wrist. That's why he felt such painful cold. And a ghost touching the corporeal world felt even worse pain. He registered the grimace on Drummond's face, and he noticed the agonized scream coming from his mouth.

He tightened he arms, pulling up against Drummond's hold, until he managed to scoot his legs up the stage. Once his free hand clasped onto the wood, he yelled, "Let go! Let go!"

Drummond released him and soared around the room flapping his hands as if he had touched a burning stove. Max rolled away from the pit, cradling his wrist against his chest. At least the icy pain crawling along his arm made it easy to ignore the fiery pain in his side. Edward's fist had nothing on Drummond's ghost touch.

After a full minute, Max sat up. "Thank you."

Drummond cinched his tie and tipped his hat. "That's what partners are for." He blew on his hands. "Let's not do that again, though. It's one thing to touch the world for a few seconds, but I had to hold you for a long time. Felt like hours."

Massaging his wrist, Max nodded. "You certainly woke me up, though. I don't think I'll be sleeping for days after that."

"Considering Wallace here will be waking up, too, we might want to get you out of here."

Max stumbled back up the theater, into the lobby, and out to the parking lot. Twice, he had to pause to catch his breath from the hot stabs his wounds formed under his skin. As he settled into his car and sent another wave of pain through his body, he worried he wouldn't be able to drive. At least, the theater was close to home. Fifteen minutes, at the most.

No. Not home. Sandra would be at the office and his mother would be at home. Better to go to the office.

As they headed onto University Parkway, Drummond leaned his head back. "I don't know what's worse — Edward getting the better of us or knowing that the moron might try again."

"He won't try to convert me again. But he'll keep trying to take over."

Max watched the road, winced at the bumps, and attempted to clear his mind. Wallace would not be stopped by talk — that much was obvious. Other than killing him, nothing they could do would stop him from claiming what he thought of as his birthright. Plus, he had a powerful witch at his side. Not a good combination to fight against.

He shook his head. Office, first. Get patched up. Then figure this out. Max's eyes drifted closed until he felt that terrible cold pass through his body.

"Stay awake, Max. At least until you've made it to the office."

Max shivered and focused on the road. Get to the office. That was the important thing. Keep the eyes open and the hands on the wheel. Just like Jim Morrison suggested. *Great. Now I'm taking advice from a dead, drugged out singer's lyrics.*

Max shivered again.

Chapter 16

AS SANDRA FINISHED WRAPPING MAX'S SIDE, Drummond concluded his tale of Porter woe. Max didn't feel up to recounting the afternoon's events, plus he held an icepack against his swelling mouth. It only became necessary to speak during the part that Drummond had spent underground.

"At least your ribs survived," Sandra said. "I'm wrapping them in case I'm wrong, but I think you'll be fine."

Drummond said, "I doubt any of us will be fine until we stop Edward Wallace."

"Including yourself in that statement?"

"If Edward is telling the truth, then Abagail Wallace is somewhere in the Other. I think it's clear that she is — who else would have sent those lackeys after me? I know I have my fair share of enemies in the Other, but those guys were hired goons and that smells more like Wallace than any of the ghosts I would expect to come after me. The fact that she hasn't followed up on it is the troubling part."

"She's been busy plotting her family's rise."

"Maybe. If we're lucky, it means that she doesn't have as much control or as much of a following in the Other. If we're unlucky, well, we all know witches like this aren't going to let something as pesky as death get in their way."

Max dropped the icepack into his lap. In a flash, Sandra had swiped up the icepack and pressed it against Max's face until he took over. She put away their first aid kit and said, "I think the first thing we need to do is —"

The office door opened. Jammer J and Mrs. Porter walked in. She barely glanced at the office, her focus resting directly on Max.

"Mother? What are you doing here?"

"You didn't expect me to come when I heard my son was injured? What kind of mother do you think I am?"

As Sandra stood, she whispered in Max's ear, "Sorry. I called J so he wouldn't worry if we ran late. He must've told your mother."

Mrs. Porter dropped her coat across Sandra's desk as she walked up to Max. Looking over him, she made a tutting sound with her tongue. "I hope the other guy looks worse."

Max grinned, then grimaced. "Ow. I did okay."

"Okay?" Drummond said. "How about a little credit over here?"

She sat next to her son and started unwrapping his bandage. "Whoever did this doesn't know anything about first aid. Don't you worry. I'll do it right so it doesn't unwrap while you sleep."

Max averted Sandra's eyes. No need. He could feel the fire roaring from her gaze as she burned a hole through her mother-in-law.

With the confidence of an old hand, J strolled across the office and reached over one arm of the couch. They had a mini-fridge there acting as an end table. J pulled out a can of soda, popped the top, and guzzled half of it. He then plopped onto the couch and belched.

As she reworked Sandra's efforts, Mrs. Porter looked around the office. "This is nice here. Cozy. You should be doing all your work here, instead of bumbling about and getting in fights."

"I didn't intend for it to happen."

"I didn't say you did. But you have to face the truth, and I'm sure your wife will agree, that you are not a born fighter."

Drummond laughed. "You got that right."

"I pay attention," she went on. "I've listened to J talk about your work. I've seen what kind of research you do. You're getting involved with dangerous people when you should be keeping your head in your books."

Max said, "I get paid to put my head in those books. But often the people paying me are looking for dangerous information. That's why they come to me instead of looking it up themselves."

She finished with his bandage and handed him a shirt. "Well, I don't like it."

"Neither do we, but it pays the bills."

"That's not true — not the bill part, the liking it part. You do like it."

Max pointed at his ribs. "You think I like getting beaten up?"

"Don't be childish. You know exactly what I mean. You like the danger, the excitement, the thrill. I see it on your face. And I understand. I do." She looked at Sandra. "This explains a lot. The two of you getting your kicks this way — of course you don't want children. That would put a sharp end to this fun you're having."

Sandra's jaw stiffened like a wolf ready to snap. "You call this fun? This is our lives. We've been harassed by these kinds of people since we first got here."

"Then you shouldn't be here. Clearly, you're not wanted."

Drummond flew next to Sandra. "Doll, let it go. I've known many people like her, and I'm telling you, she doesn't even know she's being offensive."

At Sandra's desk, Mrs. Porter shifted her coat aside to read the title of one book: *Witchcraft in Winston.* "What is this all about? Are you two dealing with cults?"

As Max buttoned up his shirt, his brain flashed red warning signs. He stepped forward, blocking off Sandra before she could react. "That's for the case we're working on. There's a group that's into witchcraft, so we've been learning about it to better understand what they might be thinking. You can't think of them like a cult."

"A bunch of crazy people into witchcraft pretty much defines the word *cult.*"

"They're not crazy people," Sandra said, barely opening her mouth.

J did not move from the couch. He knew trouble when he saw it, and Max appreciated that he was smart enough to stay quiet.

Max's mother picked up the book with two fingers as if it might foul her hands otherwise. "My dear, this is a book about people who believe in magic spells and supernatural powers, Satanists who dance naked under the moonlight and perform deviant acts, all in the name of a superstition. That is crazy. And before you say another word, you need to start listening. I've been quiet out of respect for your position as my son's wife, but I can see now that I've been quiet too long."

"Oh, crap," Drummond said as he backed away from Sandra. "Max, I'm going to go do some research in the Other. If she doesn't kill your mother, consider yourself lucky." Max had no way to stop Drummond, and a second later, the ghost disappeared.

Mrs. Porter's stern posture brought to life all the years of old-school parenting she held within. She wielded it like a broadsword, ready to cut down all obstacles in her path. "It's one thing for Max to have these foolish notions, but it's an entirely different matter for you to indulge them. Perhaps your mother didn't teach you, but it's your job to hold a family together. Is that why you resist children? So you don't have to take the responsibility? Doesn't really matter. This nonsense has to stop. I mean, look at your husband. His got more bruises than a prize fighter, and yet you've shown no concern for him."

"Enough!" Sandra held her tight fists straight at her sides. "You were not invited here — not just this office but to our home. You simply showed up, and then you think it's okay to criticize every aspect of our lives. But as usual, you've got it all wrong. My husband is tougher than you know. He's great at his job, and he doesn't need you or me or anybody else to indulge him. He knows what he wants to do, and he's doing it. As for family — we are a family. The two of us and PB and J and others. We don't have to have our own kids to be whole. That's another thing — get it through your head that we are not going to have a child. I'm sorry if that disappoints you, but it's the way it's going to be. Now, if you want to remain our guest here, then you are going to start showing us some respect. We have a life that we've worked unimaginably hard to build here. You don't get to come here and piss all over it."

"How dare you talk to me like that."

"I should've said something days ago, but I care about Max enough to put up with you. I won't have it anymore. All the years you've looked down your nose at me. No more. This is my office, too. And you are staying in my home. You want to be here? You want to see your son? Then learn your place."

Both women breathed heavily, seething at each other. Max cleared his throat. "J, do us all a favor, and take my mother for a walk. Maybe you two can have dinner, too. There's a bunch of places around here she'd like."

J didn't respond, his eyes locked on the confrontation.

"J, please."

With a jolt, J got to his feet. "Okay, yeah. C'mon Mrs. Porter. Let's get out of here. Take a few hours to let things chill."

Though Mrs. Porter did not reply, she did pick up her coat. Keeping her eyes on Sandra, she let J lead the way out of the office. Once the door closed, Sandra dropped to her knees, lowered her head, and cried.

"I'm sorry, honey," she said. "I'm so sorry I did that."

"It's okay." Max slid his sore body down until he sat next to her. He put his arm around her and listened to her sniffles as she shivered against him.

For ten minutes, he held her without another word until at length, Sandra lifted her head. She dabbed at her eyes with the sleeve of her shirt. "No matter what she and I said, one thing is true. You can't keep getting beaten up. We need to focus on this case and find some way to stop Edward."

Her wet eyes pleaded with him to help her ignore the fight and pour their energy into the work. She had already said all that needed to be said. Rehashing it now would be pointless. And she was right — they had to stop Edward Wallace because Max's body wouldn't handle another assault.

"Then let's work," he said.

Chapter 17

AFTER SPENDING A HALF-HOUR staring at a computer screen, Max wanted to rub his eyes, but he resisted the urge. The pain in his face had dulled, and he didn't want to aggravate it. Instead, he kicked his feet onto the desk and leaned back causing his chair to squeak.

Sandra stayed focused on her old texts. While he had been at the theater learning about the shape of Edward Wallace's fists, Sandra had uncovered several spells for breaking other spells, but in each case, she had to know the specifics of the original before it could be broken. She then delved into numerous books boasting a Call to Power spell in their contents, but so far had come up empty with anything that sounded like what Abagail Wallace had used.

Max had spent the time searching for two important pieces of information. First, he wanted to find out the name of the last person whose cursed bones Wallace sought. Second, he needed to find out if Wallace had indeed found that person's bones.

He started by going through Chester Stanton's story to see if any of it had been true. Max pulled up newspaper articles from the time, academic papers on the subject, as well as some wonderful primary sources — Tryon's personal journals and official reports had been preserved as well as several invoices for arms, ammunition, food, and ominously enough, coffins. From these, Max determined that the general idea of what Stanton said was correct but the details tended to be wrong. There were only about eight cannons, not twenty, and while many of the Regulators had come expecting the incident to be another protest, clearly some arrived raring for a fight.

The office door opened. J and Mrs. Porter entered quietly.

She carried two take out boxes and placed one on each desk.

J said, "We thought you might be hungry, and I told her that when you guys hit the books, it can go all night. I figured if you were still here when we got back, that's what you'd be doing."

Sandra set her pen down. "You know us well." Her tone straddled a line between complimenting J and jabbing at Max's mother.

Before an argument could spiral away, Max said, "Thanks. I could definitely eat."

Mrs. Porter scanned the office. "If it's okay, I think I'll do some cleaning in here. I promise I won't bother your work, but it'll give me something to do, and the place could use it. No offense."

Sandra's fingers dug into her desk, but she forced a smile. "That would nice. Thank you."

Taking a few awkward steps toward the door, J said, "Y'all seem to have things good here, and I got to get checking on PB. So, unless you need something?"

"Go ahead," Max said, wanting to chuckle but thinking better of it. "See you in the morning."

As J left, Max opened the take out box — a turkey sandwich from the coffee shop on the corner. He tucked into the food while Sandra returned to her books. In the silence, Mrs. Porter dug a rag from under the bathroom sink and went to work.

But only a few minutes later, she said, "It's no wonder you never eat well when both of you bury yourselves in work. You've got to take care of each other. It's no fun when your spouse passes away because you didn't do the simple things like eat well."

Neither Max nor Sandra responded, and thankfully, Mrs. Porter returned to cleaning in silence. Another half-hour passed, and Max had yet to come across mention of Chester Stanton, Archibald Henderson, or Jonathan Shoemaker — at least, not the ones he searched for. There were plenty of men with these names scattered throughout the US, but none with any connection to the 1700s. He tried searching for them in some lesser known databases, but again turned up empty.

Glancing over at his wife's furrowed brow, he could tell she had not found success either.

Catching his gaze, she pointed to one of the books. "This is our best chance but it's in an old German dialect. The Internet's helping translate some of it, but most of it I have to piece together by cross-referencing similar texts I have in English. It's a real pain."

"Keep at it, hon. You can do it."

"Oh, I'll get this sucker. I just don't know how long it's going to take."

Max decided to shift gears and focus on Abagail Wallace and the Wallace family. After a few cursory searches, he learned that the Wallace family had stayed out of the news for their entire existence. Not surprising, but he had hoped some basic searches would pull up enough information on the family to be a primer.

Instead, he went by the tried and true methods of researching a family history. He started with the national census. Those searches brought up more than enough to put together a decent family tree — not all the way back to Abagail but all the way back to the start of the census. Of course, many of those listed would belong to other non-family people named Wallace, but by searching the Internet with each name, Max expected the narrowing process to go rather quickly.

It did. But not as he had expected. After two dozen names, he picked up on the pattern — anybody who had any information on their life, whether a newspaper article from 1927 or a Facebook page from 2015, anybody that Max could find did not belong to Abagail Wallace's clan. Thus, anybody who did not exist beyond an entry in the census did belong to the family. In fact, the only other documents Max could locate for a true Wallace were birth announcements and obituaries, but those were outliers rather than the norm.

Max's mother let loose a long sigh as she sat on the couch. Max glanced around the office. "Wow, Mom. The place looks great."

"Oh, no need to thank me. I love taking care of you. It's

important that somebody does."

Sandra ignored the comment, and Mrs. Porter waved off Max's rebuttal. It wasn't a dismissive wave, however, but rather one that said she did not want to argue anymore. That felt like progress.

Max checked his watch. "Another thirty minutes and we'll go."

"It's getting dark."

"Thirty minutes. I promise."

For the next twenty minutes, Max's mother sat quietly with her cell phone. Max tried to focus on his work, but he could hear every annoyed shift of her clothing, every perturbed huff, every sigh. He fought the urge to pack up and go early. This thirty minute wait had become a line in the sand, and if he budged, he would lose.

It had happened before between them.

Growing up, lines like this one formed on most days. Their battle of wills could ignite over anything. As a toddler, when his mother demanded he get ready for kindergarten, he stalled as long as possible, pushing her but always relenting short of getting spanked. As a boy, he refused to eat what she required, frustrating her but always relenting short of getting sent to his room. As a teen, he rejected his chores, angering her but always relenting short of getting grounded.

He could not relent this time. He was an adult, and he had a job to do. This time she had to be the one to give in.

As Max battled this out in his head, his mother meandered around the office. Nine minutes left. He sifted through papers and brought up a few historical websites. Busy work, of course, but at least it looked like work.

She slid a chair over and sat opposite him. He glanced at her. She offered a humble smile.

Not going to work. Eight minutes. *I'm staying the full thirty*.

He sensed her leaning forward, reading his papers upside-down. And then she made a slight sound. "Huh."

Max dropped his hands on the table with a loud slap. "We'll leave in a little over five minutes. Please, let me work."

Mrs. Porter cocked her head to re-read one of the papers. "Oh, I was only wondering why, back in the 1700s, well, why did they make more coffins than they needed for a hanging?"

"What?"

"That page there says they hanged six men after this battle, right?"

"That's right."

"But I thought I saw the order for nine coffins to be made. That's a lot of work when you already know you only need six."

Max's heart jumped a beat before racing away in his chest. He picked up the invoice for the coffins. Sure enough, the order stated nine coffins to be made. With frantic energy, he rifled through his notes.

Sandra lifted her head at the sudden flurry. "You have something?"

Smacking a paper with the back of his hand, he said, "Right here. Thompson and Sons."

"Which is what?"

He looked from his mother to Sandra. "They made the coffins for the six Regulators hanged after the Battle of Alamance. Only, as my mother pointed out, they made nine of them. And right here is the business register of companies and employees. Tryon needed these lists for taxes. Guess who built those coffins."

"I'll go out on a limb and say the name Wallace popped up."

"Andrew Wallace."

Sitting straight on the edge of her chair, Mrs. Porter said, "Who's that? Did I solve the case?"

"No, Mom. But you helped us with a big part of it. Andrew Wallace made three extra coffins so that his wife, Abagail, could use them for a special spell. She planned —" Max froze as his mind pulled several pieces of the puzzle together. "The men that she buried with the cursed bones — they were never Regulators. Or if they were, they didn't fight in the Battle of Alamance."

Sandra snapped her fingers. "She used the battle as cover."

"Exactly. She murdered the three men or had them killed or

maybe they sacrificed themselves, but the battle was used to hide their deaths. Just three more in the massacre. That's why I can't find their names in anything about the battle. They were never part of it."

Drummond shot out of the bookcase as if he had sprinted in from far off. "Not quite."

As Drummond perched near the front door, Max got to his feet. "What do you mean?"

"I know who the third man is, and he did fight in the Battle of Alamance."

"Do I have to guess?"

Drummond paused long enough to make Max think the answer was *yes*. But then the old ghost pushed back his hat and said, "Chester Stanton."

"But —"

"The guy we talked with in your car wasn't Stanton. That guy's name was Theo Russett and he lived in the 1950s. Abagail Wallace threatened to curse his living family if he didn't take on the Stanton role and guide us to the theater."

"How did you find this out?"

"I'm a detective. And a good one, too. Things weren't adding up right, and I had a hunch that it all seemed to break down with Stanton. So, I went back to the Other, tracked him down, and got him to tell me the truth."

"He just blurted it out? Isn't he worried about his family?"

"I may have made a few promises about what we can do to help him, but that's for another day. Right now, we've got to go talk to the real Stanton."

"You found him, too?"

"That part was easiest of all. Abagail had targeted Theo Russet for a specific reason — the guy was a historian. Care to guess what time period he specialized in?"

"The American Revolution."

"That's the one. Even stuck as a ghost in the Other, Theo couldn't stop his historian brain. He'd been interviewing those that remained from the 1700s for his own personal satisfaction."

"He knew exactly where to find Chester Stanton." Max perked up. "The details he told us — some of them were wrong by a long shot. Was he dropping us hints?"

"I think so. He didn't put up much resistance when I found him." Drummond clapped his hands together once. "So, Stanton's never left the battlefield. Should be easy to find him. Let's go."

The adrenaline rush that always came with a major leap forward in a case now flushed through Max's system. He whirled back to his desk to get his coat. Sandra stood behind her desk, her face ashen as she watched Mrs. Porter.

Max's mother stared at him with a horrified gasp. "Why are you talking to the wall?"

Chapter 18

MAX'S CHEEKS REDDENED as he faced his mother. He needed a lie, a good one, anything that would make even the slightest bit of sense, but her eyes stopped him. She was scared. Her little boy might be going insane right in front of her.

Sandra burst out a sharp laugh and quickly covered her mouth. "Oh, I'm sorry, but I've told him for years somebody would think he's nuts. The idea that it's you is too funny."

Confused, Mrs. Porter moved her head an inch toward Sandra, but her eyes stayed on Max. "What are you jabbering about?"

"Max isn't crazy. That's just the way he does his best thinking. When we were younger, he'd be out mowing the lawn, yapping away at nobody. He's thinking out loud, that's all. But I've always said to him that our neighbors were going to think he'd lost his mind."

Max forced a guilty grin. None of that was true — they had never even owned a house with a lawn until moving to Winston-Salem — but he had known people who talked out their thoughts. Maybe Sandra's lie would work.

"Good thinking," Drummond said.

But Mrs. Porter shook her head. "I heard him. That was not talking through a problem. That was a conversation. He paused to listen to his imaginary friend talking." To Max, she said, "Who do you think you were talking with?"

"No, Mom. It's like Sandra said. I was thinking through our case."

"You're not well, dear. I should've known when I first got here. I did know. I ignored all the signs. Your constant distraction, the way you were running off all the time on this big case, but it's not true. None of this is real." She walked across the room and clasped hands with Sandra. "I see now that you've been dealing with this a long time. I had a friend, Ernie Schleffer, very nice man. But he wasn't right in the head either. Thought he spoke to tiny creatures in the forest. His dear wife, Sylvia, she spent years indulging his fantasies in order to keep him out of an institution."

Sandra said, "That is not what's going on here."

"It's okay. I know we've had our differences, but I see the stress you've been under. You're not in this alone anymore. You don't have to play along with his fantasy."

Drummond paced near the door. "I think your mother is the nutcase. Does she really think you're paying for this office and going around taking clients that don't exist?"

Max went to his desk and tapped on the files. "Mom, I'm not crazy. The case is right here."

"Of course, dear. You sit down and get back to work on your case. It's about witchcraft, right? Magic spells? Did you have a breakthrough on the culprit?" She turned back to Sandra and whispered, though loud enough that Max heard anyway, "I know people up north, professional people, who can help Max. Please, allow me to bring him up there. You come, too. We'll get him all the care he needs."

Sitting in his chair, Max watched on. His heart warmed at how his mother handled what she perceived as the destruction of her son's mind. She wasn't crying or yelling, but rather, she truly wanted to get him care. She behaved quite admirably.

Sandra, on the other hand, had shifted toward anger. The more Max's mother insisted on helping, the more she refused to accept Sandra's plausible explanation, the angrier Sandra became. "No," she finally said. "I'm not sending Max to an institution. He's not crazy."

"You're not hearing me. I know the truth. You don't have to hide it from me anymore."

"You are so far off base from the truth, it'd be laughable if it wasn't so dangerous."

Drummond soared over to the desk. "Max, I think you better stop them."

Max wanted to say something back to Drummond about self-preservation, but he guessed that talking to the empty space next to him would only fuel his mother's convictions.

"Please, dear," Mrs. Porter said as she closed in on Sandra. Her attempt at an understanding and sympathetic face chilled Max. He couldn't imagine Sandra liked it any better close up. "The only danger is letting Max continue to be sick. He needs a doctor — a trained professional."

"You amaze me," Sandra said.

Drummond pointed toward her. "Don't do this."

"You come to us uninvited, barge into our lives, and after only a couple days, you think you understand the world we live in. You think you can understand my life. The arrogance that takes."

"Arrogance?" Mrs. Porter said, the edge coming back to her voice. "Now, you listen here. I can see that times have been rough for you, but I'm trying to be nice. There's no need to be insulting."

"It's insulting that you think you can dictate what Max and I want to do — especially when you don't have a clue as to what is really going on here."

Max got to his feet, his brain finally clicking in to what Drummond feared. "Honey, it's okay. Let's not bring all that up."

Mrs. Porter's eyebrows lifted. "You two are hiding something else? Is his condition worse than talking to imaginary people?"

Pounding her fists on the table, Sandra said, "He's not crazy!"

"It's obvious that you are in denial."

"It's a ghost. Okay? You want the truth? Max was talking to a ghost. A dead detective that Max and I can both see. In fact, he's right over there."

Mrs. Porter looked in Drummond's direction. Her lips trembled, and her hand went to her chest. The way her eyes darted from Max to Sandra and back spoke for her — she thought they both had lost their minds. Which left Max with no choice.

"It's true, Mom."

She bit back a few attempts to speak.

Sandra nodded to Drummond. "The ghost is going to pass his hand through you, and you'll feel it. It's cold. Try not to freak out."

Drummond drifted behind Mrs. Porter and raised his hand. He glanced at Sandra, and she nodded again. Max watched that pale hand descend, and he wanted to scream.

This part of his life should never have been revealed — certainly not to his mother. This part of his life belonged between Sandra and him. It was private, personal, something that he did not want shared with anyone but his wife.

Yet Sandra was right. Better his mother thought him cursed, better she was scared into believing the supernatural, than to have her trying to lock him up in an asylum.

Drummond swiped his hand across the back of her shoulders, and she yipped like a frightened poodle. She whirled around to stare at her empty chair. "W-What was that?"

"I told you," Sandra said. "A ghost."

Max put his arm around his mother's shoulders and directed her to a chair. "It's true. There really is a ghost."

"A ghost?" Mrs. Porter said with glazed eyes. Her look gave Max an uncomfortable view of a dementia patient — lost and confused, trying to grasp onto anything familiar. She placed her hand on Max's cheek. "I don't understand."

"I know. You don't have to. Just know that I'm not losing my mind and neither are you. Okay? Everything here is fine."

Drummond leaned near the bookcase. "Might I suggest some medicinal fortitude?"

Thinking he could use some himself, Max pulled out one of Drummond's fake books and removed the whiskey flask hidden inside. He snatched a plastic cup from the bathroom and poured his mother a stiff drink. Then he tipped the flask back for a quick shot himself.

After two helpings, Mrs. Porter began to calm. Her color returned, and her face grew stern. "I'm not going to pretend that any of this makes sense, but perhaps I'm too old to figure out the way you young people do things. I don't get how the Internet can do so much — and apparently it can play tricks on an old person's nerves. Look, as long as you're okay, that'll have to do."

"I am fine, Mom."

"Then we're all good," Sandra said. "It's been a long day, and from what I could make out of Max's brainstorm, we've got a long night ahead of us."

"Yeah, that's true. We need to interview a man in Alamance. It's a bit of a drive from here. I'm sorry, Mom, again. I really hate how these days are turning out for you."

She fluttered her hand as if shooing away a fly. "I feel quite tired. I think I'll go back to the house and call it an early evening."

"Sounds like a smart idea," Sandra said. "Plus, you'll be there when J gets back. He shouldn't be too late."

Max escorted his mother out of the office and down to the street. He gave her the keys to his car and sent her on her way. When he returned, Sandra had already shut down the computers and put away their papers.

She pocketed her keys and looked to Drummond. "Well, where exactly do we find the real Chester Stanton?"

Chapter 19

DRIVING ALONG ROUTE 62, Max sat in the passenger seat and attempted to pull himself together. "I can't believe we told my mother about ghosts."

"You'd rather she cart you off to a nuthouse?" Sandra said.

Sitting in the back, Drummond said, "The two of you need to forget about that. It's done. You can handle the situation with her in the morning. We've got more important problems right ahead."

On either side of the road, the zigzag pattern of split-rail fencing could be seen under a near full moon. The battlefield stretched off in both directions. Back in 1771, the fencing would not have been there but the road was — not paved, of course, and named the Hillsborough-Salisbury Road. Sandra drove straight through to a driveway on the left with a metal-bar gate. She parked parallel to the road and shut off the car.

Moving her head slowly, she surveyed the area. "Strange. Not many ghosts here."

"Should there be?" Max asked.

"It's a battlefield. Lots of painful deaths, youth cut down early, violent deaths — yeah, there should be a lot of ghosts."

Drummond said, "Not here. Most have moved on."

"Oh, yeah. I'm still not used to thinking about ghosts that way."

After scanning the area, Drummond went on, "One of the few ghosts here should be Stanton, and he ain't one of the Brits, so that narrows it down some."

Max looked over his shoulder. "You don't know what he looks like?"

"I found out he's here, didn't I? I'm the one who got the information. It didn't come with a photo. You're the research guy. Why didn't you find a picture of him?"

"Okay, okay. Point taken."

Drummond readjusted his hat. "Look, I'll go out there and chat up those ghosts until I find Stanton. Then I'll come get you two. So, stay here."

"I'm not sitting in this car for another hour while you roam around. We'll be on the battlefield. I don't think you'll have a hard time finding us. This place isn't that large."

"Fine, fine. Can I get to work or are you going to talk a dead man into his grave?"

Saying nothing more, Max gestured for Drummond to be on his way. Once he left, Max shared a glance with Sandra and they both chuckled. They got out of the car and walked around the gate — it was not designed to keep anybody out, just to discourage cars from driving in.

Max checked the road — nobody had come by since they had arrived. If they were lucky, the road wouldn't be heavily traveled this late on a weeknight. Feeling the sore bruises on his flank reminded him not to feel too lucky.

They walked up the drive to a visitor's center on the left. Max didn't bother trying the doors — they would definitely be locked this late at night. Instead, they strolled around the building to a concrete porch at the back. An 18th-century cannon had been situated with its barrel pointing out into the fields.

Max marveled at the small but powerful weapon. The actual metal body only measured a few feet. Most of the weapon consisted of a frame made of thick, heavy wood, and two large wooden wheels with metal treads lined with square rivets for traction. An angled information table sat to the right of the cannon. It bore a map of the battlefield, showing where Governor Tryon's men had lined up — mostly straddling the road to the left of Max's current position — and where the Regulators had set camp — in a wooded area straight ahead and to the right.

Standing next to the cannon, Max pictured the scene from so long ago. Tryon's men stretching down the line. They were not actual "redcoats" but rather North Carolina militia men conscripted by Tryon, so they lacked the discipline of formal soldiers. Yet they had sided with the British and wanted to impress the Governor. They would be at attention, ready to act, perhaps even eager to attack.

On the other side, a rabble of men and boys thrown together out of necessity. Government corruption had reached the point where it could no longer be ignored. After years of pleading and arguing and compromising, of being promised change that never came, of watching the dreams provided by this bountiful land squandered under the greed of a few, the Regulators could take no more. They were here to protest, and no amount of posturing or bullying from Tryon would stop them.

"Honey." Sandra's voice raced him back to the present.

He patted the cannon. "It's amazing, isn't it? This all happened right here. The seeds of the American Revolution were sowed right here."

"I'm sorry. About your mother. All of it. I'm sorry. I don't know why we can't get along. I don't think she's ever tried to like me. And, well, I tend to bite back when somebody comes at me like that."

Max hugged her and pecked her cheek. "I'm sorry, too. Not just about my mother."

Her arms tightened around his waist. She smelled of shampoo, and Max wanted to forget the ghosts, the case, and his mother, and simply go home with his wife for a quiet night together. Too often, they did not get enough time to spend curled up and in love. Too often, work and bills and life forced them into non-stop patterns of behavior that led to misunderstandings that led to fights.

"It's a good thing we're married," she said. "Otherwise, I'd probably have killed you by now."

He snorted a laugh. "The police would find me with a knife in my chest, but my hands would've been locked around your throat."

Muffling her amusement in his chest, she said, "And we

both would have had guns pointing at your mother."

They held each other a bit longer, until finally, Max broke away. He squinted into the moonlit field. The ground sloped downward slightly, and it appeared that a large rock sat at the head of a shallow gully. The ghost pretending to be Stanton had mentioned that before.

"Come on," he said. "I want to check that out."

The rock poked up in the middle of a grassy area. As he came closer, Max thought it might be three rocks pressed against each other, but he couldn't be sure. Several feet away, Max saw another angled information stand. He walked over and, using the light from his cell phone, he read:

Pugh's Rock

According to legend, Regulator James Pugh, brother-in-law of Regulator Herman Husband, lay behind this rock while he fired on Tyron's troops.

The sign went on to suggest that rumors of James being one of the six men later hanged in Hillsborough proved false because records indicated James signed a will in 1810. Most likely, his brother Enoch, also a Regulator, died in 1771, perhaps even one of the hanged.

Max crouched behind the rock. He could see the cannon quite clear and close. "The guts a person would need to take this position."

"I'm glad they eventually got to move on," Sandra said. "Anybody who died here, facing that kind of thing, would be twisted up for sure."

"Aren't we waiting to meet a ghost like that?"

Even under the moon, Sandra appeared to pale more. "I know."

"Hon, if this is too much for you, we can turn back. We'll find some other way to get the information. Drummond can talk to this ghost without us or I can —"

"That's sweet but not necessary. All I'm saying is that we need to be prepared. This ghost, it might not be as easy to deal with as Drummond."

Max sat back on the rock. "Since when is Drummond easy to deal with?"

"I heard that," Drummond said as he approached. "I'll have you know that in my day, many of my lady friends would vouch that I am a charming and easy-going fellow."

"I've met one of your *lady friends*, remember? Led a witch coven to possess my wife and tried to destroy us. Real nice gal."

"Hey, we all make mistakes. She's not the only woman I ever dated."

Max held back further comment because he saw the way Sandra gawked at the air behind Drummond. He saw nothing, though. "Did you bring Chester Stanton with you?"

"Of course. I said I was going to get him."

Max brushed Sandra's arm. "Honey? You okay?"

She nodded, but her stunned expression did not agree. "I've never seen a ghost like that before. He's all — I don't know — he's shredded."

"Shredded?"

"He's mostly bones like a skeleton but with his flesh and clothes hanging off in shreds. It looks like moss and vines hanging from tree limbs. And he's weirdly tall. Maybe seven or eight feet." She turned to Drummond. "What did this to him?"

Drummond made a bitter face. "That's what happens when a ghost breaks the tether keeping him close to where he was cursed."

Max cringed at the thought. He had seen it with Drummond and experienced it when cursed into a coma. The tether — a set distance a ghost could move away from his curse. If he went too far, his body stretched painfully as if an actual tether strained to pull him back. It never occurred to Max before that a ghost might be able to snap that tether, break free, and no longer be bound by the curse. Picturing Chester Stanton as Sandra had described him, Max decided the ghost traded one curse for another.

Drummond pursed he lips. "From what Theo Russet told me, Stanton took a bullet here on the battlefield, and Abagail

Wallace must have pretended to aid him. She then cursed and carved his bones, letting him die out here. Don't know what she had against him to do this, and so far I can't get Stanton to talk. I figure he didn't like being a ghost, so he broke apart his tether which ripped him into this. He probably spent some time by his old home or following his family or maybe his mind got shredded too, and he wandered around lost and confused. Eventually, he found his way back here, trying to find his body, I guess."

"Shouldn't he have moved on?" Max asked.

"I don't know. This is the first ghost I've ever seen like this. Maybe breaking free of his tether also broke him free of the Other. Maybe he can't be forced to move on, and he's too disoriented to figure it out himself."

Sandra grabbed Max's hand, her skin clammy and cold. She whispered. "He has no nose, no eyes — just the dark holes of a skull."

Nothing could have frightened Max more than seeing Sandra disturbed by a ghost. She had been seeing ghosts most of her life. They were part of everyday existence. For Stanton's visage to unsettle her this much, he had to be more than a horrifying sight. She had to see his anguish.

As best as he could, Max pushed away his mounting fear. To Drummond, he said, "He can't be too confused. He's here. You were able to talk with him and bring him over to us. So, he can comprehend a few things."

"He knows his name. He knows where he is. But I don't know how much of this he understands. We might only be an interesting distraction."

"Let's not wait until we're no longer interesting. Ask him if he knows where his body is buried."

Drummond complied, listened to a response, and said, "He wants us to follow him. At least, I think that's what he's trying to say."

"I think so, too," Sandra said. With a sharp motion, she dropped Max's hand and walked back toward the cannon. Max had seen this before — Sandra regaining her impressive strength. She had a moment of doubt, and then, through sheer willpower, she shoved aside her fears and refocused on solving their problems.

He jogged up next to her. "I love you, hon."

Were it daytime, Max would have been sure that she had blushed, but at night, he could not see clear enough to know. Still, he felt the warmth between them rekindle, and that told him more than any words or look she could provide. He also saw the determined focus in her eyes. She had work to do tonight, and she intended for it to be done without fail.

She pointed off to the right of the visitor's center toward the road. "Stanton's going that way."

They crossed the street onto the rest of the battlefield. Two small monuments had been built on the field. The first, encircled by shrubs, consisted of an obelisk atop three square blocks of stone. An inscription read: *first battle of the American Revolution.*

"Arguable," Max whispered, "but close enough."

He followed Sandra and Drummond further across the grass towards the second monument. Like the first, this one bore a tall pillar atop three square blocks, but instead of coming to a point at the top, this one had a statue of James Hunter, a Regulator leader who survived the battle only to be outlawed in the aftermath. Two plaques had been secured to the sides of the monument, but Max could not read them in the dim light. As he brought up the flashlight app on his phone, Sandra and Drummond continued on.

"This isn't it?" Max asked.

Drummond waved him to follow. "Does it look like we're stopping?"

They approached the tree line, and Max saw two signs. One read: *Alamance Battleground Walking Trail.* The other: *Nature Trail. No Admittance when site is closed.*

Passing by the signs, Max knocked on the trunk of a nearby oak. He figured he could use all the good luck nature offered at the moment.

The trail wound through the woods like a maze. At times,

the path opened wide enough for them to walk side-by-side. A few sections, they had to go single file. Sounds of crickets, frogs, and other nocturnal creatures filled the air with clicks, clacks, and croaks.

Up ahead, Drummond stopped, and Max assumed that meant the ghost of Stanton had also stopped. The path went off to the left and right, but even without Max's flashlight, he could see that the path reconnected and continued on further up. The idea that the path formed a circle did not seem so strange, except there was nothing in the circle — no old tree that need to be preserved, no historic marker to suggest something important, not even a treacherous pit to be avoided. Nothing.

"Is this where you're buried?" Sandra asked the empty space ahead of Drummond. "Then what is it?"

Drummond glanced back at Max. "He shook his head *No.*"

"Thanks, but I figured that part out."

"Just trying to help. If you don't want to know what he's doing, I'll save my breath."

"You know I'm not saying that. And you don't have breath."

Drummond winked with a sly grin. "Joking around, that's all. Stanton's floating in the middle of the circle, and he's got his arms out but I don't get what he's trying to say. Sandra?"

She said, "I don't know, either."

"Let me see," Max said, moving to the front. Nothing about the area stuck out as odd or noticeable. Trees, rocks, ferns, and moss — nothing special.

"Um, Max," Drummond said. "You better step back."

"Why? What's going on?"

Sandra tugged on Max's sleeve. "Stanton is moving toward you. He's got his hand out — I think he wants to tap into you."

Max stumbled back. He had been through that before. A ghost could place its hand in a person's head, and as long as they remained connected, that person would then see all that the ghost sees. But it hurt like a quadruple migraine. So far, Max had survived the experience, but he felt confident that if a ghost lingered too long in his head, the chances of dying skyrocketed.

"No, thank you," he said to where he thought the ghost approached. "We'll figure out what you want here. No need for that."

Drummond flew in front of Max and pointed at Stanton. "Look, pal, he ain't interested. Besides, I'm a ghost, too, and I don't see anything here. So, Max won't see anything either."

"Duck!" Sandra said.

Drummond's head cocked to the side and his body flew off to the left. "What're you hitting me for?"

Fearing the ghost might act like a bear and pursue the flight of a terrified animal, Max fought the urge to sprint off into the woods. The temperature of the air near his face dropped. His breath puffed out as if on a winter's eve. His mouth trembled, not from the cold but from the unnerving knowledge that somewhere in front of him, a ghost reached out with a hand full of frozen pain. His heart hammered. His tongue dried. The shaking of his breath filled his ears.

With a guttural cry, Drummond charged across the path and tackled Stanton. "I'll hold him off. Go!"

Max flung Sandra around, clasped her hand and tore back up the path. Twice his feet rolled on loose stones, but he managed to stay up and running. Sandra soared along next to him, never once faltering.

When they broke out of the woods, they did not stop. They dashed by the monument with the statue and went straight for their car. Sandra thrust her arm forward, holding the car keys like a dagger striking an unseen assailant. The car beeped twice and flashed its lights.

They yanked open the doors, jumped inside, and slammed the car shut. Sandra turned over the engine and screeched the tires. As she pulled onto the road and sped away, Max's phone rang. They both hit the ceiling and screamed.

The scream morphed into laughter as Max dug his phone from his pocket. "It's my mother," he said, and Sandra laughed harder. Letting his shoulder drop as he squished back into the passenger seat, he slid his finger across the phone. "Hi, Mom.

How are —"

"Max, you've got to come back. Quick."

Hearing his mother's quivering voice shot the tension right back into his shoulders. "Why? What's wrong?"

"I'm so sorry." Her voice cracked. "I couldn't stop them. They barged in and I'm too old. I couldn't stop them."

"Calm down. Is anybody hurt? What happened?"

"It's J. They came and took him."

Max's heart stopped. "What do you mean? Who took him? The police?" Both PB and J had boosted cars and done other illegal things in order to survive the streets. It wouldn't surprise Max if that came back to haunt them at some point.

"No, not the police." She cried out the words.

"Then who? Calm down. You're not making sense." But she was making sense, and he knew it. His mind simply didn't want to admit it. He had to hear the words from her mouth to confirm what the twisting of his stomach already had accepted.

She complied. "A bunch of men. They burst in here and took him. Do you understand? J's been kidnapped."

Chapter 20

MAX HAD SEEN SANDRA DRIVE FAST BEFORE, seen her weave around cars like a professional driver, seen her press the gas pedal to the floor and flex her fingers around the wheel, but he had never seen her push a car with the determination that blazed in her eyes when she heard that J had been abducted. If a police car had flashed its lights behind them, Max thought his wife would surely ignore it. She would let every patrol in the area chase them and let every helicopter spotlight them — nothing would stop her.

Drummond appeared in the backseat. His suit had been ruffled up as well as his hair. "That was interesting. I never thought old Stanton would have tried to tap your head. Maybe Sandra would've liked you better that way. What do you think, doll? A vegetable Max would be a lot easier to deal with in the mornings. Hey, not to tell you how to drive, but you're going a bit fast."

Max ignored the crude comment and instead brought the ghost up-to-date on what happened with J. "I need you to run ahead of us. Get to the house and watch over my mother."

"Shouldn't I go find J?"

"No. In all likelihood, Edward Wallace took him. If that's true, he'll want to use J as a bargaining chip or a way to control us. If that's not true, then J was taken by strangers. Either way, we should end up getting a ransom call or some other kind of demands put on us."

"What if he was taken by some sicko monster, and we only have a short time to save him?"

"I've thought about that plenty already and there's not much we can do, if that's the case."

"But I can —"

"You can zoom ahead of us, but then what? He could be anywhere. He might have already left the state, and then later, the country. So, let's focus on the outcomes we can do something about. That starts with you getting to our house and watching over my mother. We'll be there soon enough with Sandra behind the wheel."

Drummond scowled at the situation, but he did head off for the house. Max called his mother again. His chest tightened hearing her so afraid.

"There were four of them. They all wore hoods except one — he had an eye patch. He said I should tell you that he could have killed me if he wanted to," she said, her voice quivering. But then a sharp edge cut into her tone. "These are those cultists you're dealing with, aren't they?"

"Don't worry. We're going to handle this."

"It is those cultists. You don't want to admit it. That sweet boy has been kidnapped because of your stupid case."

Sandra cut across two lanes for the exit, garnering a long, angry honk from a silver BMW. She swung around the ramp and onto Silas Creek Parkway. Nighttime traffic remained light, but they still had to contend with several possible red lights up ahead.

"Hold tight, Mom. We'll be there shortly."

"I should call the police. I can't believe I didn't do that, yet. You get here soon, but I'll call —"

"No, Mom. Don't. The kidnappers might kill J if we get the cops involved." He hoped that was more a lie than anything, but he also believed that Wallace would be angry if the police were called, and that would only exacerbate the situation.

"Then what should I do? I can't sit here and do nothing. Oh, that sweet, sweet boy."

"Ten minutes. We'll be home that fast, and then we'll figure it out. Please, sit tight, don't call the police. Just wait for us."

Without a response, Mrs. Porter cut the call. Max made a fist and punched the car door. "Can't we go any faster?"

They reached their home is less than eight minutes.

Max had the passenger door open before the car had

stopped. He raced up the walk and only stopped at the sight of the front door. The framing had been split by a large force — the same force that knocked the door off one hinge and blasted the deadbolt clear through the wood.

As Sandra hurried up the walk, Max headed through the door with caution. It had only been eight minutes, but that much time could be more than enough to do serious damage. Eye-patch might have returned, attacked Max's mother, and hauled her off to some dark location which would make a work camp seem like a day at the beach.

But when he entered the house, Max heard his mother busy in the kitchen. The furniture in the living room had been tossed around, but the hallway, stairs, and dining room all looked untouched. He approached the kitchen like a nervous spelunker in a volatile cavern, each step taken with the expectation of disaster.

"Oh, good, you're here," his mother said as she caught sight of him entering. She had on a flowery apron that Max had seen in the pantry many times but neither he nor Sandra ever wore. With her hands in constant motion, Mrs. Porter bustled about the kitchen — baking cookies while brewing coffee.

"Mom?" Max said in a gentle tone reserved for keeping unstable people stable. "Why don't you have a seat?"

She flashed a smile at him that looked more terrified than joyous. "That's sweet, dear, but I don't have the time. I have to get things ready."

Drummond dropped through the ceiling and swished across the room. "I was beginning to think you two had met with an accident — or worse."

Sandra pushed by Max and glanced in his office. "Everything's okay in there."

Forcing another smile, Mrs. Porter said, "Everything is okay everywhere. We just have to get things ready and it'll all be okay."

Drummond crossed his arms. "Sorry, Max. She's been like this since I got here."

Sandra returned to Max's side. "This was Wallace. They

came in specifically for J. No other rooms are touched. They didn't comb through the office or anywhere else to steal anything. They wanted J and nothing more."

Mrs. Porter opened the oven enough to peek in, then slammed it shut. "Why steal a little boy? It doesn't make sense." She covered her mouth, and tears dropped over her fingers.

"Probably leverage," Max said. "We'll have to wait until they contact us and make demands."

Sandra ushered Max aside. Whispering, she said, "There's another possibility."

Swooping in, Drummond said, "Oh, I don't like what you're suggesting."

Keeping her voice low, she said, "Why else would they take J and not bother with her?"

"Damn. You're probably right."

Max smacked Drummond's shoulder, but his hand passed through. "One of you, tell me what you're talking about."

Sandra tapped the inside of her forearm like a heroin addict. "Blood. I've been searching everything I could to find something about that spell. But I didn't look into the worst, darkest magic — blood magic."

"You think they took J for his blood?"

"He's young, and despite his bragging, I'm pretty sure he's still a virgin. My guess is they took J to hurt us a little, but mostly because he's full of young, virgin blood. That's powerful stuff."

"You're saying he's going to sacrifice J?"

Drummond said, "He's got all three bones, and now he's got this blood. What else does Wallace need?"

"How should I know?" Sandra whispered loud enough for Mrs. Porter to look up from her bowl of cookie dough. "I haven't found the full spell, have I?"

"But you know what spells need, in general."

"So do you. So does Max. Candles, a circle drawn with the right symbols, sometimes fire, sometimes earth. But the specifics — you got any idea what else this spell needs?"

They didn't have time to escalate into a full argument. The

doorbell rang.

"Finally," Mrs. Porter said, untying her apron. She set it over the back of a chair and primped her hair as she walked to the front door.

"Wait," Max said. "What do you mean *finally?* Are you expecting somebody?"

"You said not to call the police, but you didn't think I'd just sit here and do nothing."

"Oh, no. Who did you call over here?"

She trembled. "The only friend I have."

Mother Hope stood on the porch with a warm smile.

Chapter 21

MAX HAD SAT IN UNCOMFORTABLE SITUATIONS BEFORE — he once dated a girl who had a crush on the bartender at the bar she insisted they go to, he once sat through a church service with terrible gas that kept bursting out no matter how he tried to hide it, he once watched his wife drink too much and start juggling oranges at a party of uptight managers — but he could not recall nor imagine anything that could touch the gut-churning discomfort he now faced. In the living room of his home, he watched as his mother served coffee and cookies to Mother Hope. Both women perched on his couch — both short enough that their feet barely brushed the floor. Sandra chose a chair on the other side of the coffee table. She could not hide her glowering stare. Max sat on the ottoman in front of her chair while Drummond hovered by the window.

Max's knee bounced up and down. "Shouldn't we be out there searching for J?"

"Hey," Drummond said, "that's what I said."

"Don't be rude," Mrs. Porter said in a strong but polite snap that most parents master early on. "I have complete faith in Mother Hope. If she thinks we should take this slower, then that's what we'll do."

"Thank you." Mother Hope sipped her coffee. "First, I promise that J is fine. Scared, surely —"

"Of course."

"— but fine."

"Oh, that's a big relief." Mrs. Porter used the corner of her napkin to dab at her eyes.

"Don't start celebrating. He's fine for now, but he won't be by tomorrow. The men that took him are dangerous, but I give you my word, I will do all I can to find your boy and bring him safely home."

Mrs. Porter patted Mother Hope's knee. "You are a true friend. There are people I've known my whole life that offer a fraction of what you are doing, and we've only known each other a couple of days."

"I feel a kinship with you. Perhaps it's because I've had some dealings with your son."

Max wanted to storm across the room and give a few more dealings, but instead, he looked out the window and waited for the ridiculousness to end.

Setting her coffee cup on the table, Mrs. Porter gave a strong nod for everyone. "Well, then. It looks like we have an ally. What should be our next step?"

Again, Max had to force his emotions down. Whatever his mother thought she faced, she had no clue what the real situation was nor how to deal with it. He might have been impressed with her gumption if not for the gnawing truth that she had shown more affection for Mother Hope and J — two people she had known for only a handful of days — than she ever had for him or his wife.

Mother Hope bit into her cookie and quickly washed it down with coffee — Max's mother had never been a good baker. "For now, you'll have to wait. I know that's difficult, but I need you to stay here and trust me. I will have my people scour the city. Even if we have to go all night and strain to see into dark alleys under the light of the full moon, I promise we will succeed. That boy is not weak nor is he a coward. He will cause a lot of trouble for his captors and that will help us."

"Of course, you're right, but I wish I could do something. It's hard to sit here. This isn't even my home."

Mother Hope perked up and regarded Max, but he refused to be baited. "There is one thing you can do," she said. "It's a strange thing, though."

"Anything. Tell me."

"These men belong to a cult, so they think and act accordingly."

To Max, Mrs. Porter said, "I told you these cult-types were

no good."

Mother Hope went on, "There are certain ceremonies that go back centuries. I believe these men will sneak back here later tonight to watch over you, to make sure you don't do anything they don't like. If they were to see you performing one of these ceremonies, it might frighten them into thinking you are a powerful witch."

"A witch?"

"Or a priestess, maybe. I don't know exactly how their disturbed minds work. But I do believe you can fake them into thinking they have dug a deep well of trouble and that it would be better off to return the boy than harm him."

Mrs. Porter straightened her blouse and fidgeted with the edge of the couch. "I wouldn't know how to do anything like that."

"I'm sure one of Sandra's books could help."

Max braced for a tidal wave of rage to explode from his wife. He expected she would rise to her feet, jab a finger into Mother Hope's chest, and yell about how she knew Mother Hope would not help them at all, that the entire Magi group had caused this untenable situation, and how she would do all she could to see them pay for any harm that comes to J. But the fiery assault did not occur. Instead, Sandra's focus on Mother Hope intensified as if she had discovered a unique mammal in the jungle and wanted to observe its behavior.

"Well," Mother Hope said, pushing at the back cushions to stand, "I should be going, if I am to find that boy. Please, don't worry. I'll see that it all works out."

As she walked to the door with Mrs. Porter close behind, Max scooted ahead of them. "Allow me to escort you back to your car," he said. "My mother raised me well, and I'm happy to ensure your safety."

"That's kind of you."

Max held back a smirk at the wariness in Mother Hope's voice. He liked the idea that she felt unsure — might even be a new emotion for her. It also meant that she did have vulnerabilities. A truly invincible person would never pale at any threat.

They walked out to the drive and toward her silver Mercedes. One of her thugs — the one that went by Trevor, the one whose fists Max had become too familiar with — leaned against the side of the car.

"Why are you lying to her?" Max asked Mother Hope, stopping halfway to the car. Her bodyguard took notice, but she waved him off. "Why are you pretending?"

"I'm not lying to her. I want to see J survive."

"You don't care about him."

"That is true. But I care about what happens if Edward Wallace gets his way."

"Then why not tell us what we need to know? How does it serve you to keep us in the dark?"

Mother Hope lifted her head so that the moonlight glinted in her eyes. "You seem to have the mistaken impression that you are vital to me. Let me make things clear. You are nothing but a tool for my use. I gave you a task — to get those bones — and you failed. And you wonder why I keep you in the dark. I have more trusted souls dealing with Wallace. The best thing for you to do is exactly what I told your mother. Sit down, shut up, and wait."

She turned to go, but he wrenched the old woman back. Trevor stepped closer, preparing to pound Max into the ground. Mother Hope held out her hand to stop him.

"You listen to me," Max said. "If you ever talk to my mother again, if you ever pretend to be her friend, I will destroy you."

Mother Hope made a small noise of indifference. "You are so forgetful." She poked his chest with a sharp finger. "That curse on you means I am the one to tell you what will and will not be done. Now, stand back. There is serious evil hatching tonight, and this city needs competent people to fight it."

She pushed him aside and shuffled to her car. As Trevor held the door open for her, he thrust his chest out, attempting to look dignified but coming off as a fool. Clearly, Mother Hope thought so. "I can take care of my own door. Get this car going already."

Before Trevor started the car and drove off, Max had spun around and stormed back to the house. Inside, he growled his exasperation. "I swear, every damn day I'm thinking we would have been better off with the Hulls."

Drummond tisked. "Grass is always greener, huh?"

"Hey." Sandra snapped her fingers at the ghost. "We don't have a lot of time. Go read that book I opened for you."

Caught up in his own frustration, Max had missed the changes in the house from when he left. He now saw that his mother had gone upstairs while Sandra had dug into three dusty volumes. One, a large tome made of old parchment and small handwritten script, lay open on the ottoman. Drummond flew over and read the text. The other two, heavy and old but smaller and printed, spread across Sandra's lap as she scoured through page after page.

"What's all this?" Max asked.

Sandra glanced up. "Didn't you hear a thing she said?"

"I heard all of it. If we don't find J tonight, he's probably going to be hurt bad, maybe even killed. And Mother Hope wants us to sit on our hands while my mother is supposed to put on pantomime of being a witch."

"I swear, honey, sometimes you're thick."

"What? What did I miss?"

"Mother Hope practically begged us to take care of this, and she gave us the key information we needed."

Max looked at the front door as he thought over all the old woman had said — including her threats outside. "I don't know what you're talking about. What did she say?"

"She confirmed that the three bones were the core of the spell, that they needed J for his blood, and then she told us that this kind of spell could only be cast under a full moon. Which is tomorrow night. That's why J is fine until tomorrow. She also told me to check all my books, that the spell I'm looking for should be in one of them."

"She said all that?"

"Absolutely."

"Why didn't she just say it plain and simple then?"

"I think she didn't want to upset your mother."

Drummond said, "I think she just likes being a manipulative hag."

"Well, there's that, too."

Max put out his hands. "Okay. How can I help?"

"Go to your study and grab *Spells of the South* and that grimoire we took from Drummond's old girlfriend." Back when Drummond lived, he had fallen in love with a woman who turned out to be part of a witch coven. The grimoire contained all the private rules and spells of the coven. Beyond that, Max didn't want to recount that harrowing case. The book would be enough of a reminder.

When he returned with the texts, Sandra said, "Look through for any spell or mention of a spell dealing with blood, bones, or the full moon. Then we'll have to read over each one until we find what we're looking for."

From the stairs, Mrs. Porter softly cleared her throat. The team's frantic energy froze as they all looked up at her. She said, "Full moon's tomorrow?"

Max swallowed hard before saying, "That's right."

Mrs. Porter came back into the living room. "Then show me how to help."

Too stunned to speak, Sandra handed over a tattered book.

Chapter 22

HOURS. TOO MANY HAD SLIPPED BY AND STILL NOTHING. Max would peek at the digital clock on the bookshelf, note the time, and then catch himself checking it again to find that an hour had gone by.

Mrs. Porter kept coffee brewing like a drug dealer making sure she had a steady supply for her insatiable customers. Max and Sandra downed the hot caffeine boost over and over. They bounced from book to book, double-checking each other's lack of findings, and all the time knowing that J's life rested in their hands.

Whenever possible, they had Drummond read through a text. Turning pages caused him pain, but Max noticed the ghost enduring in order to keep the process moving along as fast as possible.

"How about this one?" Mrs. Porter asked, bringing a volume of *Common Spells and Practices* over. Sandra glanced at the spell, shook her head, and returned to her own research.

In addition to reading through page after page, any translations needed to be done were handed off to Sandra. Max wished he could help more. After all, he had been tagged with the role of brilliant researcher. However, in this case, he could only be the assistant. He knew a lot about witches and witchcraft but not nearly as much as his wife.

Making the process even more frustrating, they had come across several possible spells that looked promising; however, there always turned out to be something wrong to discount it. Some spells lacked the need for blood. Some could be performed under any moon condition. Some required rare ingredients that would have taken colossal effort and risk to acquire. Max happily researched if any of those ingredients had been brought into the United States but found no declarations or murmurings to suggest so. Of course, they could have been smuggled in, so those spells were set aside for further consideration. But Sandra's lack of enthusiasm for the possibility suggested they were grasping for any solution rather than the one that would work.

Tired and wired, Max used the bathroom off of the kitchen. When he finished, he found Drummond waiting for him by the sink. Out of habit, he glanced at the stove clock — 4:07 am.

"You find something?" he asked.

Shushing Max, Drummond moved in close and spoke low. "I'm worried about Sandra."

"Shouldn't you be worried about J?"

"Really? You're going to be word picky and sarcastic now?"

Max rubbed his sore eyes. "Sorry. Been a long night. What are you worried about?"

"She's acting obsessed. That can be bad at any time, but in a situation like this, it can be dangerous — to her, to you, to all of us."

"Of course, she's obsessed. We all are. The clock is ticking and we've still got nothing to stop J from being killed. How do expect her to act?"

"She hasn't taken a break other than to use the bathroom, and that's only been once. All night. Whatever we're going to face is less that twenty-four hours away. We can't afford for her to breakdown from pushing too hard."

"If we don't push hard, then what? We fail and J dies."

"I know what's at stake. I'm only saying —"

"What? What is it you want me to do?"

Drummond removed his hat and floated back to the counter. "Back when I was starting out as a private detective, I had this one case — Gene Holston. He came to me because he had experienced something he could not explain. A lot of my business started that way. Became pretty obvious that his house was haunted, and I was surprised that he accepted the truth about ghosts quite quickly. I tried all the basic things but couldn't clear the house. That's when Gene started reading up on the subject."

Max glanced toward the living room. "I take it your friend got a tad obsessed."

"He wouldn't stop. Night after night, he would read until bleary eyed and dazed. He quit his job so he could spend his days at the library. He wrote letters to psychics and visited gypsies at traveling carnivals. I tried to talk sense into him, tried to force him to slow down, even brought in an exorcist despite the fact that nobody was possessed. Nothing got through to Gene. Nothing. Until he found a book on witchcraft. He decided to fight fire with fire. One night, he went into his basement and attempted to cast a spell for calling upon dark powers."

"I take it he didn't succeed."

"Oh, he did. He brought up a terrible, evil spirit that destroyed the ghosts haunting his home. But he failed to first cast a spell to contain and control that evil. It killed him." Drummond turned away. "Gruesome sight."

"I'm sorry about that, but Sandra is not Gene. She has plenty of knowledge about this stuff."

"No." Drummond spun back. "She's only starting to learn. And the point wasn't that Gene didn't know better. The point is that he was so obsessed with his goal that he overlooked what should have been obvious to anybody reading that book. Sandra knows more, but that extra bit of knowledge coupled with obsessive behavior could mean disaster. She'll assume she knows what she's doing and can easily miss something crucial."

"But she's not alone. We're here."

"All the more reason to worry about her. If this all fails and J dies, she'll be devastated. The kind you don't bounce back from. You understand?"

"You think she'll snap? She'll need to be hospitalized?"

"I don't know. I don't have an answer. I'm just trying to get you to see what's happening, to be aware of it, and help me keep an eye on things. If you got a better idea, I'd love to hear it."

Max locked on Drummond's cold eyes. Neither spoke. The

problem floated between them, and Max had no answer. Pushing hard, pushing through a problem — they had survived and then defeated the Hulls that way. It took a certain amount of obsession to be focused enough to succeed against a coven of dead witches or a house built with traps and spells or a ghost witch. And now, Drummond expected them to back off?

Sandra's excited cry cut through the silence. "Everybody come here!"

Max and Drummond thumped into the living room to find Sandra and Mrs. Porter sitting in the middle of the book piles. Sandra, disheveled and red-eyed, beamed at Max with such pleasure that he smiled back. He knew that look well. He had worn it many times doing his own research. The joy of discovery.

"What do you got?" Drummond said as he settled above the group.

Sandra lifted a well-kept copy of *Oddities*. Max raised an eyebrow. The book had little to do with witchcraft and everything to do with deformities, mutations, and strange talents of people throughout history. To clear up Max's confusion, she thumbed the book open to a page about a third of the way in and held it out for all to see.

"Right here," she said. "Handwritten notes in the margins."

Max leaned closer. He couldn't read the words, he didn't know the language. "What's it say?"

"*Aufruf an die Stromversorgung*. It means Call to Power."

"That's the actual spell?"

"No. It's notes on the spell. Ingredients, which we already know — bones, blood, full moon — but it also says here that the spell needs a ceremonial casting."

"Is that what it sounds like?"

"Pretty much. You can't just cast a ceremonial spell. It needs the energy created from a group performing a specific ritual. From what I can make out here, the group needs to be at least five people around the edges of a natural circle."

Mrs. Porter said, "How is a natural circle different from a regular circle?"

"It's formed by nature, so it may end up being more of an oval or a raggedly-shaped circle. More circular than anything else. An eddy might form into a natural circle. A bird's nest is usually a natural circle, though that would be too small for this spell."

"This cult, then, needs a large open area. A clearing that happens to be shaped like a circle."

"And according to these notes, the space has to be a *land der toten* — a land of the dead."

"Maybe a cemetery?"

"Oh, crap," Max said.

Mrs. Porter slapped the back of Max's hand. "Watch your language."

"Sorry. But I know where this ceremony is going to take place." Even as he spoke, Max saw Sandra's eyes widen as she understood. He glanced up at Drummond and saw the realization hit the ghost, too. "That's what Chester Stanton was trying to show us. The Call to Power is going to happen at the circular clearing near the Alamance Battlefield. It's a swatch of land where many died."

Drummond clapped his hands together. "We've got the advantage now. They don't know that we've found them. Let's go."

"Hold on. We can't go running in there half-cocked while they still have J." Max caught his mother trying to ignore when he spoke to a ghost she could not see. He appreciated her silence for the moment, but at some point, he expected she would want more of an explanation. "We need a plan."

Sandra tapped a book on the pile to her right. "I've got one. Now that we know the Call to Power is a ceremonial spell and a few of its key details — at least, I hope they're the key details — I know what spell we need."

"You found a way to stop the spell?"

"Not exactly." She flipped through the pages of the book. "It's called the *Rite of Dark Passage*, and we can use it to help us with what I have in mind."

Drummond soared over to the door. "Fine, then. We've got

a plan. Can we go?"

"It's not even dawn yet," Max said. "Wallace can't do his spell until tonight under the full moon. We should get some rest and prepare."

"No," Sandra said. "Drummond's right. We need to get going now. Our spell will take time to cast. I'll explain the whole plan on the way."

Drummond winked. "Doll, you're the greatest."

"You're only saying that because I agreed with you."

Max went to grab his car keys only to find his mother standing with them jingling in her hands. "What are you doing?"

Clutching the keys into a tight fist, she said, "There is no way I'll be left behind in this. I may not believe half of what you're saying, but I know that sweet boy needs our help. All of us. So, you can waste time arguing with me and losing that argument or we can get moving."

Max never got a chance to answer. Sandra walked right up to his mother and put out her hand. "I expected you to come along," she said. "But Max is driving."

Mrs. Porter looked Sandra in the eyes, and Max worried the two might come to blows. But then, his mother dropped the keys into Sandra's hand. The two women shared a quick nod before heading out to the car.

Chapter 23

As Max drove toward the Alamance Battlefield, Sandra explained her plan — at least, as much of it as she had worked out. They were going to check over the battlefield in the daylight and locate a suitable area to perform the Rite of Dark Passage. By the time they set up their part, Edward Wallace and his cult should arrive, and all would be ready to go. Drummond's first job would be to observe and report what went on with Wallace, J, and the Call to Power while he waited for Max, Sandra, and Mrs. Porter to cast the spell. Then it would all be up to him.

"Drummond shouldn't go in there alone," Max said. "Wallace isn't some feeble fool. Even without the Call to Power, he has some ability. Don't forget, he used magic to pull those coffins from the ground."

Sandra did not look up from the open book in her lap. "Not much choice. We need three people for the spell, and in this case, Drummond doesn't count."

"Hey, I count plenty." Drummond crossed his arms in the backseat next to Mrs. Porter.

Max appreciated that the ghost took care not to accidentally pass through his mother, but she looked discomforted anyway.

She poked the back of Max's shoulder. "I know you believe in this ghost stuff, and I understand that this cult really believes it, but I still don't think this is the best way to save J. Fighting pretending with pretending is not going to stop them from truly harming him."

"Mom, I can't argue this anymore. You are going to have to trust us."

"I'm trying. But —"

Sandra turned around and leveled her stern eyes on Mrs.

Porter. "J means more to us than you'll ever know. Do you honestly believe that we would jeopardize his life on a hunch of pretending? Do you think that low of your son?"

"I don't think low of Max at all. But sometimes he makes rash decisions, and I simply —"

"You're scared, right now. We understand. We've had to deal with this kind of thing before and it is scary. But we need you to tap into the Porter strength that keeps you going because we need you. Without your help, there is no doubt in my mind that J will die. The police won't believe any of this, and even if they did, there's nothing they can do."

Mrs. Porter crossed her arms causing Drummond to shift his posture. With half-hearted effort, she muttered, "They could arrest Wallace before he has a chance to hurt J."

"That's true," Max chimed in. "But that wouldn't stop anything. Wallace has been planning this for years and his family has planned for centuries. They have certainly factored in the police. Mother Hope, too. They definitely factored in her. In fact, they've got to have contingencies for their contingencies. There's only one thing that they might not have planned for."

With a defeated sigh, Mrs. Porter nodded. "Us."

Except for the turning of pages in Sandra's book, the car remained quiet for the rest of the drive. When they pulled into the parking lot at Alamance Battlefield, a minivan parked next to them. A haggard father with two children got out and walked towards the visitor's center.

"Good," Sandra said. "We won't look suspicious with them around. We'll be nothing more than another family checking out the battlefield."

Max opened his door. "Sure. As long as you leave the book on witch spells in the car."

The area appeared quite different in the daylight. Sun filtered through the trees and a lovely breeze fluttered the grass. Max found it difficult to imagine the torrent of noise, the blood-soaked cries, and the vicious mayhem that occurred during battle.

Before Max could get around the car to join his mother and Sandra, Drummond said, "Well, we're here. What do we need to do first?"

Sandra pointed to a small log cabin with a sharply inclined roof off to the right. "Let's start there."

"But the trail to the circle is on the opposite side of the road," Max said.

Mrs. Porter headed toward the house. Without looking back, she said, "Sandra's in charge, so let her be in charge."

Sandra put her hand to her face as if struck. "I think that's the first time I've ever liked your mother."

Gesturing to the house, Max said, "You sure you still want to go there? I've no doubt she'll find a way to ruin your new-found feeling toward her."

Taking Max's arm, they followed Mrs. Porter. Drummond drifted nearby.

"We need a good location on the battlefield to cast our spell," Sandra said. "As long as we can see the opening to the trail, we should be fine."

Max glanced over his shoulder. "I don't think that house is going to help, then."

"It'll be different at night."

"Yeah, darker."

"But it's really Drummond that'll need to do the seeing, and a ghost can see things you can't."

Floating backwards so he could scrutinize the field, Drummond said, "There's a dim glow in the woods. Is that what I'm supposed to see?"

"That's the energy from the circle they'll use tonight. According to the book in the car, all locations frequently used for spells start to give off a glow. The more a place is used, the stronger the glow."

"I always thought those glows were the remains of other ghosts that moved on or came to a bad end or something. Never realized they were special spots for witches. Those woods aren't glowing very much, though. Looks like it's barely been touched."

"Don't forget, you're seeing it in the daylight. The glow should be more pronounced at night."

They approached the house from the side. It had no windows, and the logs that formed the walls were all cut flat. A stone chimney rose on the far side, and the warped porch dipped in the center. Around the back, Max noted doors to a root cellar and also a second porch loaded with cut firewood.

An information table explained that this house had been built around the 1780s by a Quaker named John Allen. It was not originally on the battlefield, however. It had been built in a nearby area called Snow Camp. In 1966, the state moved the dwelling to Alamance partially to display living conditions of that era, but also because John Allen's brother-in-law was Herman Husband, leader of the Regulators.

"Well?" Max asked Drummond.

Drummond squinted into the distance. "Maybe. It's hard to tell in the daylight."

"No," Sandra said. "We're too far away. I'd hoped it would work here because of all the cover. There's not much on the other side of the street except open fields and a couple of statues."

They strolled through the battlefield, acting like tourists, and worked their way to the street. The father and his children emerged from the visitor's center. He made a half-hearted comment to his boy, but the children sprinted across the grass, screeching and giggling.

Mrs. Porter's wistful gaze followed them. "You know, it's not too late to —"

"No, Mom. We're not having that conversation today."

Sandra squeezed his hand as they crossed the street. Like tourists, they meandered across the open battlefield and stopped at the statue in the back, not far from the wooded trail entrance. Sandra shielded her eyes as she checked back across the way.

"This would be the best place for being close to what goes on inside there tonight, but it's so exposed. Anybody driving by could see us, if they happen to look our way."

Drummond said, "It shouldn't be a problem. We're doing this thing around midnight, right?"

"We do our spell whenever Wallace does his. It should be near midnight, but that doesn't mean he'll do things the right way."

"Relax. He'll do it right. Besides, he'll never get a chance because Max is going to take care of it all right now."

Max's stomach turned, but he kept quiet. He thought he saw a similar unease cross Sandra's face. That didn't make him feel any better.

"Okay," she said. "Let's get this going. We need a flat rock from the battlefield. Something big enough to write on that looks like it would be good for skipping across water."

"Over here." Mrs. Porter picked up a rock the size of her palm. "Will this do?"

"Perfect."

Sandra dug a piece of chalk from her pocket and wrote three symbols on the rock. Max recognized the first two symbols — a group of wavy lines and one that made him think of a sharply angled 'P' — but the third symbol was new. It was a circle, filled-in, but the longer Max looked at it, the more he thought it represented a skull.

Just my imagination. It's a big dot and nothing more.

"You drawing a skull there?" Drummond asked.

"Don't worry about that." Sandra handed the rock to Max. "Your mother and I will be back tonight. We'll get everything ready, and as long as you do your part, it'll all be fine."

Max took the rock and tried to ignore the way it seemed to heat up in his hand. "No problem. As long as Drummond doesn't make me crazy."

"He's not going with you, honey."

Drummond leaned his head in towards the trail. "Don't worry about it. I'm coming along at first, but then I've got a side job your wife wants me to do. I promise I'll be back before the fireworks get going."

"You better," Max said. "If you're late and anything happens to J —"

"No need for that. You know I'll be there."

From her purse, Sandra took out a garden trowel. "Take this, too."

"You think of everything." He put the trowel in his coat pocket.

"You know what you're looking for, right?"

"I'll be fine."

Sandra leaned into Max and kissed him — a soft kiss, a gentle touch that quivered underneath the skin. "Be careful."

Between the odd heat radiating from the rock and the odd timbre in Sandra's voice, Max felt a pit of worry form in his gut. The mouth of the trail called to him with a rustle of leaves. The sound, normally peaceful and pleasant, now filled his ears with dread. He wanted to hear Drummond throw off a wisecrack or two, even a corny pun would suffice, but the ghost eyed the trail entrance with as much trepidation as Max.

Placing the stone in his pocket, Max kissed Sandra — more firmly this time. Then he headed off, not daring to look back for fear that he would run straight to Sandra's arms and refuse to return to the trail. What did it really matter if Wallace succeeded? Mother Hope in charge or Wallace in charge, it made no difference.

Max shook off the thought. He was here to save J. That mattered. Why would he think otherwise?

Heat from the stone in his pocket warmed his thigh. Max tapped his fingers against his side. Could that be altering his thoughts? Could it be filling him with doubts and fears?

"I'll be happy when this is done," he said. "You ever notice that we're the two always going into the dangerous parts of a case?"

Drummond chuckled. "First, Sandra's been involved in the dangerous parts plenty. Second, you've got to accept the truth — we like the danger."

"I don't."

"Sure, you do. Afterwards. During these things, like right now, it's frightening. Maybe sometimes you have a real rush when caught up in the middle of things. But after, when you've survived, that's the real thing that we seek. That's when the adrenaline is still pumping and you can smile because the danger is gone."

Max stopped on the trail. A metal signpost to his left read:

A Regulator Moment

Some memoirs of the battle state that Tryon had a horse shot out from under him during the battle, but Tryon failed to mention this in his report on the battle.

Max said, "You think Governor Tryon was smiling afterwards because he survived that?"

"Tryon was smiling because he won the battle."

"Well, if I'm smiling when this is done, it won't be because I survived. It'll be because J is alive and I won't ever have to see Wallace's face again. Let's go."

They followed the trail until they reached the split in the path and the circle beyond. Max strained a look back up the way they had come. Trees poked and twisted like a tangled wall. He could not see the battlefield. The branches above him seemed to lace together in an effort to blot out the clouds and sun.

Drummond flew over to an overturned Eastern red cedar, its reddish-brown bark had rotted long ago, its few remaining limbs poked out from the far end, its base and roots a vertical mass of dirt and rock. "This looks like a good spot."

Humming an aimless tune to ease his nerves, Max sauntered over to the fallen cedar. Drummond was right. Max would be able to hunker down behind the trunk and nobody would see him. He had a clear view of the circle, and when the time came, he would be able to sneak around without detection.

"What do you think?" Drummond asked.

Max crossed his fingers. "I think Sandra better get everything she needs because I don't want to be stuck here for nothing." He plunked down with his back against the trunk. "Go over to the circle and make sure you can't see me."

Drummond moved away. A second later, he said, "You're all

good." He returned with an unsettled look on his brow. "That circle gives off some weird sensations."

"Under the circumstances, I'm guessing that's a good thing. At the very least, it means we're in the right place."

"Yeah. Then I better get moving."

"You have to go already?" Max hoped the pitiful sound he heard was more in his head than in his voice.

"I don't relish the idea of coming back to Sandra empty-handed. She's always been a tough gal, but since your mother has been here, Sandra's downright frightening."

"I'll let her know you're scared of her."

Drummond's chest rose. "Now, that's not what I'm saying." But the concern in his eyes did not agree with his words. "Look, we're here to save J, and I've got my part to do. You worry about your part. I'll be back later to help you out, if you need it."

He didn't wait to be baited into further talk. For a minute, Max watched the empty space where Drummond had been as if the old detective might materialize, say he was joking, and float overhead for the next few hours. But that did not happen. After it became undeniable that Max was alone, he let out a sigh, tightened his coat around his shoulders, and leaned his head against the log.

Most likely, nobody would be coming by until the park closed and night fell. Until that moment, there was no reason to expect any trouble. Yet Max could not shake the feeling that he sat in the middle of a searing skillet. He only hoped he wouldn't be soon thrown into the fire.

Chapter 24

MAX HAD RUN THROUGH THE LYRICS of his favorite Led Zeppelin songs, tried to decipher the lyrics of his favorite Red Hot Chili Peppers songs, pondered why a great band like Foxy Shazam never received the accolades they deserved, and pondered why a band like Nickelback received more than they deserved. And yet, when he looked at the time on his phone, he still had a few more hours of waiting ahead of him. His nervousness had long since departed since nothing much had happened. He did see a rabbit, but upon closer inspection, it turned out to be a rabbit-shaped rock.

Twice he considered pulling out his phone and playing Candy Crush or some other time-waster. Twice he rejected the idea. He could put the phone on mute, but he couldn't afford to get caught because of the light announcing his location like a lighthouse beacon.

In an effort to stay awake, and also out of bodily necessity, Max stood, stretched, and walked deeper into the woods until he thought he was safely from view. Then he opened his pants and relieved his bladder upon a sapling. After, he headed back to the safety behind the fallen tree, but before he reached it, he spotted a figure approaching the circle.

Max jumped behind a maple with a narrow trunk. He could hear the man's steps crunching the dead leaves on the ground. Squatting low, Max peeked around the tree. He could not see the man — which, hopefully, meant the man could not see him. Slowly, he duck-walked to the fallen log. His thighs burned with each step, and his breathing tightened. By the time he reached his position, sweat dampened his arms and back.

Peering through the rotted cedar, he finally laid eyes on the man. After having fought several of Wallace's followers, Max had imagined a burly man with a thick beard and scarred face. Instead, the man looked like a college kid. Not only young, but thin and gawky. He wore wire-frame glasses, had short hair, and sported khaki pants with a green, button-down shirt.

Had the sun still been up or had the young man not gone directly into the circle, Max might have concluded that the young man was, in fact, a college student doing research for a botany class. But the sun had set hours ago. And the young man had gone straight for the circle. There was no mistake. This kid was here to get things ready for Wallace.

Max observed as the kid walked the circle, picking out stones and twigs and tossing them into the woods. He then used his foot to sweep the leaves into a pile which he did his best to set outside the circle. Finally, he searched for a tree limb. At first, Max thought the kid wanted a good walking stick, but that proved to be wrong. Once the kid had selected the right tree limb, he consulted a wrinkled paper dug from his pocket and proceeded to use the tree limb as a writing implement. He drew a large circle on the ground and then the necessary symbols.

When the kid lifted his head and stretched, Max pressed close to the ground. A leaf vibrated from his shaky breath. He trusted the fallen cedar to obscure him from view, but he didn't want to take any unnecessary chances — especially with J's life at risk.

Like a string of squid-ink pasta shoved through a press, a black snake slipped out of a hole in the log. Its head touched the ground less than a foot from Max, and its body continued to flow out of the hole. A pink, forked tongue darted from its mouth as it slithered alongside Max. Then it shifted to the left and across the back of Max's legs. Still, its body had not completely left the log.

Max didn't dare breathe.

He watched the scaled body undulate as it moved and wished he knew how to identify a snake. The thing had to be over six feet long, and its head had an oval shape. At least, Max thought it was oval. The snake's appearance had startled him, and he already couldn't count on his memory. All he knew was that it was a snake, and that he could feel its weight crossing his legs.

Black rat snake. Max had heard of those and knew they were plentiful in North Carolina. Were they venomous? Or were they constrictors? What if it was a cobra? No — those didn't live in the United States. They were in India and Africa and maybe Australia. Everything deadly lived in Australia. Did it matter? Where the snake came from, what kind of snake it was, or whether getting killed by snake venom or getting killed by a snake crushing the trachea didn't make much of a difference. Dead meant dead.

The snake paused. Its weight pressed against Max like a firehose full of water. He closed his eyes and tried to picture Sandra at the beach. Warm, the sound of rushing waves, chatter of children playing in the surf, the smell of sunblock and fried food. And Sandra — reading a book under the sun. But the snake started up again, and Max opened his eyes to see dirt and the log and the leaf and the tail end of the snake as it continued on its way.

Again the snake stopped, and this time, Max felt it tugging at his pant pocket. Gently lifting and turning his head, Max peered down his leg. It had doubled back over itself and halted with its tongue flicking around the pocket — the pocket with the stone Sandra had inscribed. Thinking about the stone made Max acutely aware of the heat building around it.

The snake reared back and opened its mouth. Max's entire body went numb as he stared at those two small teeth that might carry his death. It swayed before the pocket, and Max thought he saw fear in the snake's eyes. The stone or the heat from the stone bothered the creature.

Don't be stupid, Max. You can't know what's in a snake's mind.

After one more cautious tongue flick of the pocket, the snake turned away. Apparently, it had decided the effort required to get in the pocket wasn't worth it. It chose an easier path — down Max's leg and back onto the dirt.

Once the last of the snake had slithered off his body, Max

gasped an intake of air. His breath rushed in with a strong vocalization, and his mind shifted to the young man at the circle who must have heard the noise. Max popped his head above the log — not a smart move but his body reacted before his mind could stop him.

Empty.

The circle was empty.

With a quick scan of the area, he saw that the young man had left. Max checked his phone — 10:30 pm. He had to hurry. The spell had to be conducted at midnight, but the ceremony would have to start earlier in order to finish on time. He fully expected Wallace and his followers to arrive within the next thirty minutes.

Popping on his phone's flashlight app, Max headed into the circle. The full moon provided plenty of light to maneuver, but he needed to find a specific symbol on the circle — three lines with jagged ends laid over each other to form a rough triangle. He found it rather quickly — it was the seventh symbol going clockwise from the northern compass point — and counted four paces toward the center of the circle.

From his coat pocket, he brought the garden trowel, dropped to his knees, and dug a hole in the ground. Sandra had told him to make it two feet deep. That sounded fine in the car but only because Max forgot how uncooperative North Carolina's red clay could be.

Slamming the trowel blade into the earth plunged the tool less than an inch. Scraping back did little more. Tiny chunk after tiny chunk, he dug. Sweat dribbled down his back from his continued efforts, and when he finally had to lean back to stretch his aching muscles, he discovered he had only managed one foot.

Resuming his labor, he wished this would have been as simple as running his shoe across the circle, breaking it open, and thus destroying the spell. That move had worked with other spells in the past. But Sandra had pointed out that Wallace would not be careless. They had to expect him to make a close inspection of the circle and its symbols to make sure everything had been done correctly. A break in the circle would be caught long before Wallace cast his spell.

The digging continued and Max's hands grew sore. "Great," he said to the hole. "Just some more pain for my bruised body."

Three thumps echoed in the distance like car doors slamming closed. Max's spine stiffened as he scanned the woods. Like an animal searching for a predator, he watched, listened, and waited while his heart pounded adrenaline deep into his body.

Beams from flashlights dappled across the trees. *Crap. They're here.*

Max threw the stone down the hole and plowed the dirt back inside to cover it up. He had to hope the two-feet measurement was never intended to be exact. With the back of the trowel, he smoothed the dirt with the rest of the ground.

Voices grew louder.

He brushed some pebbles over the hole and tossed a few leaves as well. Stepping back, he tried to inspect his work with only the moonlight. He thought it would suffice. Not that he had much choice in the matter.

He could discern approaching footsteps.

Damn. The plan had been for him to bury the stone and leave. He would then meet up with Sandra, his mother, and Drummond to cast their spell once Wallace's group had entered the woods. No way could he escape now — going back up the path meant passing by them and trying to go around via the forest meant getting lost in the dark. His phone had GPS, but he worried that the light from the screen would be like shining a giant arrow over his head. Too easy for his enemies to spot him.

New plan — hide.

Max scurried back behind the fallen cedar as the front of the group arrived at the circle. Salty sweat trickled into his mouth. Inching slower than a snail, he brought his head in position to watch through the log.

Four men, all wearing the hooded garb of Wallace's group, came forth with lit torches in hand. Next, two more hooded figures carried in a long wooden post. Finally, four people arrived — one was Wallace, two were hooded like the rest, and stuck between them, Max saw J.

The young teen tried to keep a brave face, but Max saw the terror in the boy's stumbling steps and constant searching of the woods. He had to know that Max would never give up on him. But as the men dug a small hole at the head of the circle and hammered the post into the ground, J's resolve weakened. His knees buckled.

The men kept J standing as Wallace smirked. "Starting to understand where you're going?"

J kept quiet — the hatred his eyes threw at Wallace said enough.

The torches had been placed outside the circle, and the shadows they cast danced around the ground. Max watched the area where he had buried the stone. People walked over it without ever noticing. Between the shadows and his quick covering, it looked like he would get away with that part of the plan.

But it didn't matter, if he couldn't get back to Sandra and his mother. *Where's Drummond?* How late would Max have to be before they think to send Drummond over to check up on the situation? That's all Max really needed. Send the ghost in to freeze everyone for a little while, create a little chaos, and Max could spring J with ease.

Maybe not ease, but he could certainly have a good shot at success.

The last strike on the post echoed in the woods, and the hooded figures backed away. With a silent motion from Wallace, the others tugged J over to the post. Despite J's straining, the men in charge of him showed little difficulty in tying him up like a witch ready to be burned at the stake. They wrapped a cloth gag around his mouth and backed away.

When they finished, each man stood behind one of the symbols drawn in the circle. Edward Wallace paced around the circle twice — once behind the men, once in front — before moving to the open space left for him, directly opposite the post with J. He raised his hands overhead, and all of his followers did the same.

Max clenched his fist and pounded his chin as he thought. The ceremony had begun. Still no sign of Drummond. But Wallace wouldn't wait, and Max couldn't be sure how long the whole ceremony would take.

"Tonight," Wallace said as the others bowed their heads, "we fulfill a destiny set down over two hundred years ago. Tonight, we will gain the power that has been denied our people for generations. By the blood of this child and the grace of our ancestors, we will take our rightful place at the head of all strength in this world."

He lowered his head, and in a deep monotone, he chanted. Max could not discern the words — he guessed they weren't in any language he would recognize — but it sounded menacing to his ears. Especially when the hooded men took up the chant like a group of demonic Buddhist monks. J groaned against his gag, but the chanting drowned out his sound.

Max rummaged through his pockets. He kept meaning to carry a pocketknife, and now wished he had done so. He had his keys and his phone. His phone!

As long as the firelight from the torches made it too difficult to see into the woods, Max should have no trouble texting Sandra undetected. Besides, all of Wallace's men had their heads down. Probably had their eyes closed, too.

He swiped the screen of his phone, but when he touched the symbol to text, his phone fluttered three old photos of Sandra and then went dark. He pressed the wake-up button, swiped the screen, and tried again. This time the messaging app came on, a blue box flickered along with a stripe of multi-colored text, and then it all went dark again.

Max looked back at the circle. J wriggled to no avail. Wallace had brought out a wooden bowl and held it over his head in one hand. In the other, he brandished a large hunting blade. "Blood of the innocent will shed its innocence. Blood of the pure will purify us all."

The Call to Power — if the chanting had already started

creating the spell, then the energy of the spell must have messed with his phone. Max pocketed his dead phone. He checked around him. Desperate, he even hoped to find that snake again. Maybe he could throw it at Wallace.

But there was no snake, no Drummond, no phone.

Wallace stepped into the circle. He tapped the knife against the bowl making a dull, steady beat that kept time with the chanting. J's eyes widened and all his struggling ceased.

Max had nothing. Nothing but himself.

That'll have to be enough.

Standing atop the log, Max put out his arms. "Hey! Stop!"

The chanting halted. Wallace twisted back as all the hooded heads lifted and stared in Max's direction. Even J looked over at Max.

Nobody moved. Nobody spoke. They all continued to stare as if waiting for Max to do something. So Max said the first thing in his head. "I was just passing through. You know of any good places for barbecue?"

Wallace looked like he had bitten into a rotten apple. "Get that sonuvabitch."

Chapter 25

WEAVING AROUND THE TREES, Max blundered forward. He wanted to sprint, but even with the bright full moon, there were numerous roots, rocks, and twigs that he would not see until he tripped. The men in pursuit must have had the same thought. Or they were severely out of shape, and Max didn't think he could be that lucky. But there were a lot of them, so being faster did not necessarily mean escaping — not when they could easily flank him, encircle him, or drive him toward danger like cavemen herding buffalo over a cliff.

Great. Now I'm thinking of myself as a buffalo.

The men behind him hooted and whistled, laughed and shouted. Cockiness rocketed amongst those in a group, and when that group consisted of those who would join a cult, the level of arrogance went off the charts. The taunts continued, but they misjudged their prey. Max was not some frightened victim, running for his life, afraid of what might happen should he get caught.

Not entirely.

He had a plan in mind. But, of course, it required Drummond to show up.

Twigs slapped his legs as he navigated his way down a slope. Several of the men hit the grade too fast and tumbled downhill much to the mocking delight of the others. Because they fell, a gap had opened in the rough line of men. Max darted towards this advantage and broke through, rushing back for the circle and J.

Branches cut across his arms stinging his skin. He smashed through spider webs that stuck to his face and a cloud of gnats that scattered around his head. Wallace's men had lost all their amusement. Instead, Max heard grunts and commands. The closer he came to the torch-lit circle, the more worried and angry those voices became.

Max broke through onto the trail and jumped over to the circle. With a guttural noise, Wallace leaped in front of J and spread out his arms. But Max could not stop to fight Wallace, somehow defeat the man, and then untie J — not with a group of unhinged madmen racing after him.

Instead, Max dashed away, dragging his feet across the symbols written in the ground. He knocked over one of the torches before shooting off into the woods again. The spreading flames and ruined circle had done their job well. Max could hear Wallace ordering some of his men to stay behind to help restore the spell.

Off to the right, Max glimpsed a close grouping of pines. He pivoted toward the trees, rushed forward, and slid on the needles underneath the lowest branches. The sweet pine aroma mixed with his sweat as he rolled onto his stomach and behind two tree trunks. Three men thumped right by him.

"I leave you alone for a tiny bit and look at the mess you've made." Drummond appeared halfway inside a nearby pine. "All you had to do was bury a rock."

Max frantically waved the ghost closer. Whispering, he said, "I could use a little help."

"You could use a little brains. What do you expect me to do? Go freeze every single one of them. Sure, why not? Who cares if the ghost feels excruciating pain when he does that neat trick? As long as you get out of a mess you created."

"I'm sorry. This wasn't my idea. And, no, I don't need you to go freeze them all."

"Good. Because I'm not your secret weapon. I'm your partner."

"Which is why I have a plan that requires two partners to work together."

Two more hooded figures sped by. Max clamped his mouth shut and held his breath until the men had disappeared into the darkness. Turning back to Drummond, he said, "I'm going to keep this up, it's a distraction now. I'll draw the men away again, and you go get J."

Drummond frowned. "I was only giving you a hard time."

"Promise me you'll do it. I don't want take a beating from these asses for nothing."

"That's stupid. You don't need to get hurt at all. Let me get Sandra and —"

A gravelly voice shouted, "I see him!"

Max popped to his feet. "Save J." Before Drummond could respond, Max bolted off in the opposite direction from the circle.

The calls from Wallace's men grew louder as Max attempted one sharp pivot after another. He snatched a peek over his shoulder — four of them, maybe five, swiftly descending upon him. Those hoods blocked out all facial features and that chilled Max's skin. They were like faceless corpses, re-animated and deadly. Monsters.

He broke to the right. Despite his burning lungs, he poured more energy into sprinting. The roots and rocks and other obstacles be damned — he had to stay free for as long as possible.

With a grunt, he jumped over a section of the forest glistening in the moonlight. A creek? A puddle? He didn't care. Keep running. Keep ahead.

Ignoring the cries from his brain, his legs slowed down to a rapid jog. Air grated his throat as he inhaled and exhaled too fast. He tasted salt and his vision blurred. Not enough oxygen?

His foot snagged on something dark and small — big enough, though, to destroy his balance. He flopped onto the ground, the air whooshing from his lungs, and a rock cut his cheek. In seconds, footsteps surrounded him. Rough hands gripped his arms and hauled him to his feet.

Max let his body go limp. If they wanted him to go back to the circle, they would have to drag him. And so they did.

Three of the hooded men had already begun restoring the circle. The fire had been doused and the torch set upright again. One man on hands and knees reworked the symbols into the ground.

But not all could be fixed. Max's head lifted higher as he noticed that the sacrificial post no longer held J and that Edward Wallace rubbed his temples as would a man who had suffered a harsh migraine. Drummond had done it. Max closed his lips tight to keep from cheering. He pictured Drummond soaring in with his trench coat billowing behind. He thrust his fist through Wallace's head, giving that fool the worst case of brain freeze, and then chilled J's bindings until they snapped. J still doubted in the reality of Drummond, but Max was willing to bet that the teen might have had a change of heart by now.

The men dragging Max along stopped before Wallace and bowed their heads. Edward snarled at Max. "You've really pissed me off."

Max shrugged. "It happens."

"Do you have any idea how long I've waited, how many hours I planned for this night, how much effort went into making sure all the preparations met the exact requirements of the spell?"

"You're asking that like I would care. J is free and you don't get your witch's power. I call that a double-header win."

"Such boldness for a man destined to die tonight."

"You keep trying to talk like some elevated, enlightened sage or something, but you're nothing more than a punk playing with witchcraft. I've seen real witches before. Powerful witches. Sorry, pal, but you don't have the real touch. Not at all."

Max knew he sounded far tougher than his quaking stomach felt. Learning to speak brave while facing life-threatening danger had been one of his first lessons under the tutelage of Drummond and the hard road of their cases. But speaking with confidence did not make one confident. Often enough, though, such bravado could cause an enemy to doubt — doubt a plan, doubt a weakness or a strength, doubt anything — and in doing so, make a mistake.

Edward Wallace, however, did not look doubtful at all. In fact, a malicious grin twisted his mouth. "Oh, you think you've stopped this night from happening, that you've saved the day. That's adorable." With a sharp motion of his head, he said to his men, "Tie him up."

"What?" Max sputtered as the men hoisted him to the post and lashed his hands in the back. "You can't use my blood. It's old and tainted. I'm so far from pure that it's laughable."

"Your blood may not be pure, but it is blood. It'll have to do. There is no way I will allow failure tonight."

"But if your spell needs pure blood —"

"Are you a witch? Did you ancestors spend generations exploring the Call to Power? Your blood will be fine. It won't be as easy a conduit to deal with, and I probably will not get the full benefit of power from the bones, but it will work. And that's all I need to get started."

The hooded men found their positions on the circle once more, and the chanting began again. Wallace made his way around the men as before — once in front of them and once behind — before he stepped to the space left for him. He lifted the wooden bowl in the air. With triumph blazing in his eyes, he raised the hunting knife above his head and tapped it against the bowl.

Max knew enough of witchcraft that he thought Wallace would regret this. No way would the spell work without virgin blood. Well, maybe that wasn't true. Maybe the spell would cast. Yet Max had an uncomfortable feeling that neither he nor Wallace would like the results.

Regardless of whether or not the spell would work, Max had a bigger problem. He would bleed to death either way.

He searched the darkness behind the men. Where was Drummond? He had to be there. He had to come back. But all Max saw was the darkness.

Chapter 26

THE COARSE ROPES CHAFFED MAX'S SKIN. After all the abuse his body had taken recently, the idea that aggravated skin could still annoy him made him want to laugh. If not for the intimidating blade approaching his body, he might have had the gumption to do so.

Wallace whisked the knife across Max's chest and pressed the wooden bowl beneath the fresh wound. Max hardly felt more than a sting. As his blood dribbled into the bowl, however, he watched Wallace's lustful gaze.

Max wrinkled his nose. "Ew, don't tell me you're going to drink my blood."

"When I drink this, it will no longer be your blood."

"Still, that's pretty gross. But you've got my blood. Mind if I leave?"

Wallace grimaced. "This is only the first cut. By the time we finish, you'll be too weak to care what I do with your blood. And then you'll die."

"Yeah? I'm not liking that last part."

"You're like an annoying fly, buzzing and buzzing. My men forgot to gag you." With a sharp look to his left, one of the men hurried to rectify the error.

Wallace turned his back to Max and raised the bowl of blood over his head. He chanted more archaic words before lowering his hands. Without any other cues, three men stepped forward and dropped to one knee. Each produced one of the femurs with the Call to Power written into the bone.

Max scanned the dark woods again. Nothing. He closed his eyes and pressed his head against the post. Did they rush J off to the hospital? Is that why nobody came to save him? Or were they trying to perform their ceremonial spell but got stopped by a cruising police officer? Or maybe something happened to Drummond? The only thing Max could be sure of was that his team had not abandoned him.

He opened his eyes to find Wallace pouring the blood over the first bone. "The power of ages past, the strength of family long dead, the wealth of a pure lineage, these things have been offered to me through mine. It is these things that I accept." He took the sticky, wet bone in his trembling hands and brought it to his mouth.

Max's ears popped and pressure pushed against his body. The others in the circle appeared to have experienced similar forces as they rubbed their ears and exchanged astonished gasps. With a deep snap like the hull of an eighteenth century frigate busting open, the bone in Wallace's hand cracked in two. One of the torches snuffed out, trailing gray smoke into the air.

Wallace let the bone fragments fall to the earth. He turned around, and in a swift motion, he cut across Max's arm. When he had filled the bowl with warm blood, he moved in front of the second bone. "The sacrifices of those before me, the opportunities set before me, the future that rests before me — it is these things that I accept." He lifted the second bone covered in Max's blood, and with more hunger than the first time, he brought it to his mouth.

Again, Max's ears popped and he felt the pressure on his body. Wallace's men murmured as another loud crack followed the breaking of the bone and another torched snuffed out. Though the hoods hid the men, Max had no doubt worry now creased their faces. Many of them must not have believed in this as anything more than ceremony. Like those who joined other cults, Wallace's men probably were lost souls looking for a community and acceptance. They didn't necessarily expect real witchcraft to exist.

The hood of the man offering the third bone fell back enough that Max could see his eager face, a face that spoke for all in the group, one that welcomed Wallace's ascension, one that wore a grim joy and a dark eye patch. Seeing the supernatural become a reality would only enforce the groups' belief in Wallace as a superior being. Then again, Max considered that maybe they were all just power-hungry asses who don't buy into the whole cult thing. Eye-patch certainly appeared to fit that description.

For a third time, Wallace brought his knife against Max's skin — slitting open the front of the right thigh. As the bowl collected Max's blood, Wallace brought his face close in. Max could smell garlic on the man's breath and wondered what kind of meal one would eat before such a ceremony — even as he saw his own blood stained on the man's teeth.

Eye-patch raised the femur high up as Wallace turned back. Wallace stumbled a step but kept the bowl from dropping. He soaked the bone in blood, weaving the bowl with less care, and giggled at the splashes that fell upon the kneeling man.

When he spoke, his speech slurred. "With bone and blood, with moon and fire, with friend and foe, I accept all the power harnessed before me and given freely by the grace of the earth." As he slurped Max's blood from the bone, another wave of energy popped ears and pressed skin.

The third bone split open and another torch extinguished. One man on the circle shivered. It started at his shoulders and rolled down to his knees. He yelped and shuttled into the dark woods. Two other men nodded and hurried off in other directions. Nobody chased after them. Wallace pointed at their backs and chuckled. "Some men are born to accept power while others cower in the woods."

All those who remained knelt with bowed heads. Eye-patch raised his head. "Did it work, Master?"

Master? Max didn't know what hurt more — his bleeding body or not being able to mock Wallace's sense of self-importance.

Wallace arched his head back. "I can feel it. The power of Abagail Wallace is coming to me."

All humor drained from Max's head. Once the Call to Power was done, once Wallace had all the blood he needed, Max knew there would be one final strike with that blade. With three strong tugs at the rope bindings, he hoped to break free. But they held firm.

Wallace set his hands on his hips. "All your efforts," he said to Max, his behavior still drunk on blood and power, "did not get you anywhere. That's the problem with the Magi and the Hulls and whatever you are. You all think you can beat me, but you aren't just fighting me. You fight my whole history. My family."

Max did not pay close attention. His eyes fixated over Wallace's shoulder on the pale figure that appeared outside the circle. Drummond.

"Something's wrong," Drummond said.

Max said, "You think?" But through his gag, nobody could understand him.

"That stone was supposed to call Stanton here. I haven't been able to find him, and the Rite of Dark Passage is almost done."

Max looked toward the trail. Did he see firelight in the distance? Sandra, his mother, and J! They must be casting the spell.

Wallace shuddered. "Oh, more. Yes, a little more, and it'll be done."

Drummond moved into the circle. "I don't like the sound of that." He made a fist, and though he still winced in expectation of the pain, he threw a punch at Wallace.

But it never landed. Drummond flew back as if shocked by a high voltage jolt.

"What was that?" Wallace turned in a circle.

Max strained against the ropes, but they wouldn't give. Of course, they wouldn't. He had tried that several times to no avail. He needed to think. Fast.

Wallace had gained some power but not all of it. And he didn't know how to control it or what it even did — otherwise, he wouldn't have been confused by the protection it afforded him against Drummond. Could that be used against him?

"Max," Drummond said as he shook his head. "Get Wallace away from that stone. I've got to dig it back up. The circle or Wallace or the dirt — something is blocking its call."

Yes, yes, that sounded possible. Max glanced at the ground. Wallace stood directly over where Max had buried the stone. Max tried to inch his foot closer to the stone, but he couldn't get anywhere near it. His feet were bound too tightly to the post.

Wallace placed the blade tip under Max's chin. With a flick, he cut upward, taking a small gouge of skin as the knife sliced through the gag. With a blood-stained hand, Wallace yanked the gag away. "I want to hear you beg and scream as you die."

Max ignored Wallace, turning his head toward Drummond. "Get in here and dig up that stone."

Pausing, Wallace glanced at the empty space Max spoke to. "Who are you talking to?"

Drummond said, "He's standing on it. You just saw what happened. I can't push him out of the way."

"He can't see you. Get the stone from under his foot."

"But —"

"Trust me. That stone will stop him."

Wallace's face tightened. His eyes dropped to the ground. "What stone?" Leaping back, Wallace pointed at the disturbed earth. "There's something buried in there. Everyone look out for this bastard's partner."

The hooded men all faced outward as Wallace dropped to the ground and dug a hole with the blade.

Drummond smiled. "Clever."

"No," Max said. "Leave it alone." He thought he sounded melodramatic at best and ridiculously fake at worst, but Wallace only dug faster as if Max's voice were a riding crop hitting him harder with each syllable.

"Ha!" Wallace sprung to his feet, holding the stone while glaring at Max. "You thought this could hurt me, didn't you? You thought you'd disrupt my spell. But look at me. The power of generations continues to flow through me. It makes me stronger and smarter. And now, you'll see the great power that I have — I will crush this stone and then I'll sever your throat."

Drummond glanced up. "About time you showed up." To Max, he said, "Get ready. I don't know what I'm going to be like if this works." He reached out and grabbed Stanton.

Like the howling of a hurricane, Drummond yelled. All of Wallace's men turned toward the noise. Drummond's body stretched upward and he screamed. The air smelled like burning plastic. Chester Stanton appeared next to Drummond, holding his hand as he stepped toward the circle.

Max lost a few seconds to shock. Sandra had described Stanton, but what Max had imagined never prepared him for the horrible sight. Everything on Stanton had been stretched and shredded. Even his teeth.

Wallace's men scurried to the opposite side, and Max pulled himself back to the moment.

He leaned toward Wallace. "I know you want to kill me." He jutted his chin toward Drummond and Stanton. "But they may have something to say about that."

Chapter 27

PALE GHOST-LIGHT STROBED against the trees and faces and the circle. Drummond's body continued to stretch until he reached the same elongated height as Stanton. Wind blasted outward as their hands melded into one object. Max shuddered at the ghostly chill.

Drummond tilted his head back, mouth open, but made no sound. However, Stanton took up where the detective left off. The shredded ghost hollered a deep, mournful moan. Their arms swelled — the elbows and forearms and biceps, all at the same time, all spreading out until they connected with each other. Drummond wailed while the skeletal Stanton dripped ghostly flesh into a mist. They were merging into one being.

Though his chin quivered, Wallace threatened, "Begone demon!"

The heads of Drummond and Stanton curved toward each other. Drummond continued to yell while a horrid hissing emitted from Stanton. More pale light flashed. Several of the hooded men covered their noses against the putrid odor — the same burning plastic but now mixed with a rotting stench like dead mice stuck in the walls of an old home.

Wallace's followers gazed up at him, waiting for him to do something effective. He narrowed his eyes and brought his hands together as if in prayer — the blade held between his pressed hands. "Abagail Wallace, I call upon the power you have placed within me. Give me the weapons I need to vanquish this beast before me."

"Oh, come on. Did you rip that off a B-movie?" Max said, hoping to break the man's concentration, but Wallace paid him no attention.

But the cult leader's focus did break. Not due to Max, but

rather due to the chanting heard in the distance. Max craned his head toward the sound. That flicker of light in the distance — the fire surrounded by Sandra, his mother, and J — it grew brighter. And the soft chanting grew louder.

No. They're coming here.

As Drummond and Stanton continued to bridge the gaps between them, Sandra approached the circle holding a tray with a ceramic bowl. Not just any tray — the ugly serving tray his mother had given them for a wedding gift. A concoction of wood, charcoal, and spices burned in the bowl. Mrs. Porter and J flanked either side of Sandra, both chanting the same archaic phrase over and over.

Wallace pointed at them. "They are the ones causing this abomination before us. Stop them."

But in order to fulfill the command, Wallace's men had to pass by the Drummond-Stanton ghost. They all made slight motions to one another, but none stepped forward.

"Disgusting cowards." Wallace dropped back and brought the knife to Max's throat. "Cease your spell or I'll kill him."

Drummond-Stanton lowered his feet to the ground. They had become one being, an amalgam of handsome detective and rotting corpse. He gestured toward Sandra, and the chanting stopped — the Rite of Dark Passage had succeeded.

Wallace lifted the knife forcing Max to strain his head upward. "You've all failed. The Call to Power has been cast, and I have taken its gifts."

Placing the tray gently on the ground, Sandra said, "Then why are we all still here? If you have all the power, then why have you allowed these ghosts to materialize and combine? Why do you threaten my husband with a knife, when you should be able to smite him with a spell?"

The cult followers backed further from the circle. Only the three men who presented the bones remained close.

Wallace whipped the knife at the ground before his men. The handle wagged back and forth as he approached them with his arms out. "You doubt me? Did you not see the spell cast? The bones broke, the torches doused. I felt the surge throughout my body. I am becoming the leader you desire. I will destroy our enemies, and we will rise."

Sandra said, "Seems rather empty when you've yet to create a single spell."

"Shut your mouth."

"Now, you're being rude." To the hooded men, she said, "You cast the spell with impure blood. The spell failed." Cocking her eyebrow at Wallace, she added, "You wasted the bones. All that power is gone forever."

"Oh really?" Before Wallace moved, Max understood — the whole time Sandra had been talking and Wallace had been chastising his men, he had been casting a spell within himself. He already stood in a sacred circle. Some spells, smaller ones, needed little more.

His hand shot out to her arm, and she stiffened, her words choking in her throat. "See?" he yelled to his followers. "I do have power. Not even their little ghost can save them." To illustrate his superiority, Wallace waved his hand through Drummond-Stanton.

Except his hand stopped on the ghost's arm — Drummond-Stanton stood firm and solid. He had a body again. He looked down at Wallace's hand, met the man's eyes, and grinned as understanding reached them both.

Then Drummond-Stanton attacked.

With a war cry that sounded like shrieking crows, the seven foot ghost launched into Wallace. The pale light surrounding him brightened as he plowed Wallace into the ground. Sandra stumbled into the arms of Mrs. Porter while all but one of Wallace's men piled onto Drummond-Stanton. As scared as they were, they still had the drive of a cult — they had to defend their leader.

But one man remained. Eye-patch.

Growling, he lunged for the knife in the ground. Max had no illusions about the man's intention. He did not seek to help Wallace — he believed Wallace could handle anything. He sought one thing only — to slit Max's throat.

Drummond-Stanton writhed and thrashed. Cultists were

knocked back in all directions, but the moment they hit the ground, they bounced back up and returned to the fray. Crackling electrical sounds followed flashes of light beneath Drummond-Stanton. With his hands straight out, Wallace thrust unnaturally into the air. The men scattered and Drummond-Stanton shot high above. He hovered a moment before dive-bombing back into his enemies.

Max felt hands fumbling with his ropes. "Who's there?"

"It's me, Bossman."

"J!" Hearing the boy's voice thrilled Max, but the joy did not last. With the knife held overhead, Eye-patch rushed toward them. Max saw the blade and knew J would not untie him in time.

But Eye-patch never got far. A loud gunshot stopped him.

Less than ten feet away, Mrs. Porter stood brandishing a snub-nose revolver, smoke drifting up from its mouth. "Take one more step toward my son, and I'll kill you."

Eye-patch scowled before turning his glare onto Mrs. Porter. She motioned with the gun, holding it steady. That lack of nervousness appeared to sway him. He let the knife fall from his hand. Kicking at the dirt, he stormed off.

Max watched the man ignore Wallace and the others as he receded into the woods. How long until they would cross paths again? Then again, Eye-patch would have to survive Wallace first. Max suspected all those who abandoned Wallace would meet dark fates — especially a man like Eye-patch who should have been devoted.

Max paused. He had seen the adoration in the man's eyes, felt the depth of loyalty. Eye-patch would never leave Wallace — which meant ...

Eye-patch burst from the woods, sprinting towards Max, his mouth open and raging. He bore no weapon but his fingers, arched like claws, ready to tear into Max's throat.

Another gunshot and Eye-patch dropped to the ground. At first, Max only saw blood. Shock that his mother had fired rippled through him. Then Eye-patch hugged his leg as he rolled on the ground. She had shot him in the thigh.

With animal fury, Drummond-Stanton clamped onto Wallace's shoulders and twirled him in a circle before tossing him upward into the trees. He launched after the man, meeting him up high, ready to strike. Wallace cast another spell — a green light that flashed an instant and sent Drummond-Stanton tumbling hard into the ground. Those men still standing tackled Drummond-Stanton before the ghost could arise.

"Get the knife," Max said. J hurried around, grabbed the knife, and in seconds had Max free.

They dashed over to Sandra and his mother. Sandra hugged Max tightly. Over her shoulder, he saw his mother. She looked shaken and cold.

She caught Max watching her. "I was aiming for his chest."

J backed up to the group, keeping his focus on the fight and his knife at the ready. "What do we do now?"

It was a good question. They had failed to come close to success of the original plan, and Drummond-Stanton was in trouble. Three men kept him from getting up while two more pummeled him in the gut. Being solid had its disadvantages.

Wallace sauntered over as if he owned the ghost — that they were no more than naughty pets. Underneath his cockiness, though, Max spotted aggravation and maybe a bit of exhaustion. The fighting alone would have accounted for some tiring, but casting spell after spell might be more draining then Wallace wanted to let on.

Max huddled close with his team. "We've got to help him."

"Of course," Sandra said, "but we can't go running in there. They'd kill us before we got halfway to them."

Mrs. Porter holstered her weapon. "I only have two shots left."

"Where'd you get that thing?" Max snapped.

Sandra said, "Drummond had it hidden in a copy of *Moby Dick*."

"Of course, he did. There probably isn't a real book in our office at all."

"Can you focus?"

"Sorry." Max looked across the debris on the ground. What

could they use? The circle — no. All that fighting had broken the lines. Besides, casting a spell usually took time, especially for a novice. Sandra wouldn't be able to do much beyond the spells she had come prepared to cast. They couldn't attack — a novice witch, an orphaned teen, an old woman, and a man with more bruises than anyone should rightfully have. Not a fighting force, to say the least.

Wallace thrust his hands at Drummond-Stanton and another electrical blast shot into the ghost. Drummond-Stanton groaned as he arched violently. The charge ripped through him and into the men holding him. They screamed and tumbled back — one smacking his head against a large shard of bone.

"The bones," Max said.

Sandra hushed Mrs. Porter from asking questions. She knew her husband, knew what he looked like when his thoughts started to connect intuitively.

"Those femurs belong to the dead men from this battlefield. Or at least, from that time. The others, the majority of people from back then, they all moved on. But not these men. These men had their bones inscribed with the Call to Power against their will. Right? They never chose for this to happen. It's a curse."

Sandra saw it now. She leaned up and kissed him. "No ghost could move on while cursed."

"They're still around somewhere. They have to be. Maybe they avoid the Other and that's why Drummond never saw them."

Drummond-Stanton kicked out, swiping his foot against Wallace's legs and sending Wallace to the ground. He rose but weaved on unsteady feet.

Max cupped his hands around his mouth and yelled, "Summon your friends! Call on them. Archibald Henderson and Johnathan Shoemaker. Call them."

Drummond-Stanton faced Max and paused. His stretched skin wrinkled like a child trying to understand a new concept.

"Archibald Henderson and Johnathan Shoemaker. They want their bones back."

Wallace's men tackled Drummond-Stanton to the ground, but one arm of the giant ghost punched through. He reached up toward the sky as if attempting to grasp a hand. Wallace stumbled to his feet, holding his head while spitting blood.

He straightened, staring off into the dark. With a shaking finger, he pointed. "What's that?"

Max put an arm around Sandra and held his mother's hand. His mother pulled J against her. "Be ready to run," Max said.

Floating in from the trees, two pale figures appeared. Both were decayed creatures. One had a tricorn hat askew on his head. The other carried a musket.

Puffing his chest, Wallace said, "I've no fear of you." He closed his eyes, recited his fast spell, and shot another electrical burst at the ghosts. But unlike Drummond-Stanton, these ghosts were not solid. The blast shot through them without harm. The ghosts raced forward and Wallace screamed.

Sandra covered her mouth. "Holy crap. There's so many of them."

"I only see the two — which is weird enough for me," Max said.

"There must be twenty. Maybe more. They keep coming out of the woods."

As the two ghosts Max could see descended upon Wallace, the hooded men launched into the air, shouting as they went. Invisible hands ripped them away into the sky. And they never fell back. Max squinted as one man soared upward, silhouetted by the moon, and vanished in a puff of smoke.

Archibald Henderson and Johnathan Shoemaker lifted Wallace off the ground and floated over to Drummond-Stanton. Standing his full seven feet, Drummond-Stanton gripped Wallace by the neck and held him in the air.

"Please," Wallace whispered, unable to make a louder sound. "I promise —"

Drummond-Stanton snapped Wallace's neck. Even as Wallace's limp corpse fell, Max couldn't be sure what had happened. A full second passed before he heard the dull crack of neck bones.

Archibald Henderson and Johnathan Shoemaker faded away.

"Woo!" J slapped his thigh, but Max and Sandra did not celebrate yet. Drummond-Stanton wheeled about at the sound with no sense of camaraderie in his hollow eyes. He stomped towards them.

Sandra scooped up the ceramic bowl from the tray and held it before the group. "What was once put together must now be apart." She added a few words from another language and shattered the bowl on the ground.

Drummond-Stanton covered his face as if shielding from a bright light. Even as they watched, Max and J kicked dirt over the few remaining flames.

"Now what happens?" Max asked.

Sandra said, "They should have split apart."

"Did you forget any part of the spell?"

"No. And don't start with me, I'm trying to think."

"All I meant was —"

Mrs. Porter touched his elbow. "Let her do her job."

Sandra tiptoed closer to Drummond-Stanton. "You in there? Drummond? Can you hear me?"

The pale creature dangled his arms at his sides and sniffed the air. Sandra put out her arm, showing the back of her hand as if approaching a cautious dog. But this dog turned rabid.

Drummond-Stanton opened his mouth and roared. Max heard a strange combination of vicious hissing and guttural growls and pained cries. As the creature leaped at Sandra, Max lunged forward and grabbed her hand, pulling her away from the creature she had made.

Chapter 28

BREAKING FROM THE TRAIL and onto the battlefield, all four staggered to a halt. Breathing heavy, Max bent over, hands on knees, and coughed. "He's not following us," he managed between gasps of air.

Sandra nodded. "It's the stone. The spell I wrote on it acts like a tether. Not as strong as one's bones, but the Stanton part of him will stick close to it."

"Because he lost his tether?"

"He's been wandering, unconnected to his body, for centuries. This is the closest he has to a real connection with anything. Would you leave that just to chase us?"

Mrs. Porter said, "Okay, so he's not following us. Who cares? Let's go home."

"No," Max said. "Drummond is our partner and our friend. We won't leave him like that."

"Like what? If what you've told me is true, then he's a ghost. He's dead already. You can't save him. But I'm real. J is real. And we should get out of here before that Wallace fellow comes back with his crazy cult."

Sandra motioned forward, but Max blocked her path. He said, "Mom, we are not leaving until this is done. All of it."

"There's more?" In those two words, she became a little girl full of fear — fear of the dark, fear of the bogeyman, fear that the world might be not what it appeared. Max heard the need in her timbre — she had to find a way to rationalize all that she had seen.

J paced by the entrance to the trail. He focused on the woods, his stride strong yet cautious. "What else we got to do?"

"You saw that creature, right?" Max said to his mother.

She peered back with a haunted gaze. "Creature? You mean

that tall fellow? The one that helped us?"

"Yeah, him. We can't leave him alone in there. Um ... he'll die of exposure."

Sandra said, "That's right. We have to help him."

"How?" Mrs. Porter asked.

Max turned to Sandra. "That's a good question. Any ideas?"

"One," she said. "Chester Stanton needs to find his resting place. Even though he broke his tether, he still needs his bones."

"Why? Drummond's bones are long gone, and he's fine."

"He didn't shred himself into pieces to be free. We broke his curse. There's a difference. If Stanton can be brought to his remains, I might be able to cast an easy spell that will help him re-connect to the tether."

"But he won't go back to being cursed, would he?"

"The Call to Power has already been cast and used up. His curse is lifted because it's gone. Look how he hasn't come after us because of that stone. If it were his actual bones, he'd detach from Drummond through sheer will. He should be able to move on after that. At least, that's how I understand it."

Max closed his eyes. He wanted to sleep — for a good year or two. "Then we have to find where he's buried."

"And we have to do it tonight. We can't let people walk that trail in the morning and find him."

"Okay. Let me think." He pursed his lips as he paced back and forth. "We know that Stanton was buried somewhere on or near this battlefield. That's why he haunts this area. He's not on this open section here because he would have found his body easily out in the open."

"What if he's under one of these monuments?"

"It's possible, but wouldn't this one with the statue or even the other one — wouldn't they be like big lights signaling to him that his body is right here? Besides, this section of the battlefield was in British control. The Regulators were camped on the other side of the street, hiding amongst those trees. It's easy to get confused around trees — they all start looking the same. Maybe he can't find the tree near where he was buried."

Max tossed away those thoughts with a flick of his hand. It didn't matter which part of the field had been under control of which side. Stanton died *after* the battle had ended. Wherever he had been buried and cursed, it had to be less open to people finding him.

"What about the visitor's center or the parking lot?" Sandra said. "Maybe after he broke free, his body was paved over or built upon."

"Possibly. But that building looks the most modern. Maybe built in the 1980s or later. And it's large enough that they would have had to dig a deep foundation. I didn't come across any articles about finding bodies in the ground."

Mrs. Porter tapped her watch. "Are we going to stand out here all night? If you don't have a plan, we could at least go home where it's comfortable and think there."

Max's synapses fired off — *home*. He jogged a few steps toward the street, peering into the dark. "I know where he is."

"Then can we go?"

Whirling back to his family, he said, "Where did you leave the car? Is it far?"

"A few blocks from the park."

"Go there. You and J, get the car and park it on the other side of the street a few hundred feet down from the entrance. If any cops come by, I don't want them getting curious, so cut the engine and keep low. But be ready if we come running."

J grinned. "You want us to be the getaway car."

"That's right." True, too. But even truer — Max wanted both of them out of harm's way. They had endured enough on this case, and they couldn't really help much for the rest. As long as the rest went the way Max now saw it going.

Once they had left for the car, Sandra said, "You going to let me in on where Stanton's buried?"

Pointing off with his chin, Max said, "The John Allen House." The one-room home they had looked at earlier that day.

"But that's not even from the actual battle."

"I know. It didn't come here until the 1960s."

"Then how is that the place?"

"Because they brought it over from Snow Creek intact and set it down. There's a root cellar, not a foundation. Deep but not too deep."

Sandra gazed at the shadowy area where the house sat. "You think he's under the root cellar."

"Where else could he be on this battlefield that he wouldn't be able to find himself? And what kind of goofed-up life are we living that I can ask that question seriously?"

With a grin and peck on the cheek, Sandra said, "My kind of goofed-up life. Okay. I know when to trust your intuition. Let's go."

She started toward the trail, but Max pointed back to the road. "The house is that way."

"We have to get Drummond."

"I thought we'd go to the root cellar, and you'd cast your spell to call him over and split him."

"You thought wrong. Nothing is going to draw him away from that stone until he finds his bones."

Max's stomach tied up. "We have to get the stone, don't we?"

"Afraid so."

"Fine." He trudged to the head of the trail. "You go to the Allen House and get everything set to cast your spell. I'll get the stone. But be ready. I have a feeling ol' Drummond-Stanton won't be too happy about me swiping his precious."

Sandra followed him onto the trail. "No."

"What are you talking about?"

"We are not splitting up again. Not tonight."

"Honey, that spell —"

"It won't take long to cast. And you saw that thing we've created — how strong it is. There is no way I'm letting you go in there alone to get yourself killed."

"So we'll go in together to get killed?"

Sandra slipped her arm around him. "At least then, I won't have to hear your mother blame me for your death."

"She probably would hold that over you."

"Forever. Even from her grave."

Leaning into each other, Max and Sandra hurried down the trail.

Chapter 29

DUCKING BEHIND TWO BIRCH TREES, Max and Sandra peeked over at the circle. Drummond-Stanton clumped in one direction, stared at the ground, whacked his head with his fists, and then moved off in a different direction. He never went more than ten feet from the circle.

Not the circle, Max thought. *The stone.*

"Got any thoughts on how we're going to get in there?" he whispered.

Blanching at the idea brewing in her head, Sandra said, "Yeah, I kinda do."

"Let me guess — I'm not going to like it."

On the plus side, the plan was simple. Max had learned long ago that simple plans worked far better than complex ones. On the minus side, Sandra had to be the one to get the stone. Max hated the idea of putting her in jeopardy, but even if they switched jobs, she would be on the minus side of the plan. There was no plus-side job in this.

"Ready?" she asked.

"No. But dawn will come eventually, so we might as well get this over with."

"It'll be fine," she said with no conviction. "Just remember that Drummond is in there."

Max stepped out from behind the tree. "You hope," he said as he strolled up the path toward the circle.

At the sound of his steps, Drummond-Stanton whirled around, huffing like an angry bull. Max waved. "Hi, there. Drummond? Can you hear me?"

Drummond-Stanton leaned forward and bellowed that horrid noise that melded too many sounds together. Trying to appear confident, Max wiggled his pinkie in his ear.

"That was loud," he said. "You know you might want to consider some mouthwash. Your breath's a bit off." Drummond-Stanton reared back. "Oh, come on, Drummond. Just a little playful banter. You know, like we always do. Remember?"

Max meandered around the circle, always staying at least fifteen feet out — out of reach but close enough that Drummond-Stanton followed him, stepping away from the circle and the stone. Once Max had the pale creature with its back to Sandra, he stopped.

"Listen to me. I know you're in there, and I know you can hear me. Well, I hope all of that's true. Anyway, we're trying to help you, but it'd be swell if you helped us out, too. So, let's start simple: Drummond, my friend, if you can hear me and if you have any control, raise one of your hands up high."

Drummond-Stanton kept his hands down.

"Okay. Maybe that was too hard. Can you do anything to show me you understand that I'm your old pal, Max?"

Drummond-Stanton shouted at him in a long, ear-splitting cry. Max saw Sandra hunched over as she entered the circle. She moved slow, avoiding sticks and leaves that might give her away, but Max had a sense that Drummond-Stanton wouldn't play this game much longer. If he could get through, even for a few seconds, Drummond might help stall things, but that seemed less and less likely.

"Are you really going to keep yelling at me? Is that all you can do? Man, I thought you were tougher than that. I mean, come on, you're Marshall Drummond. Are you telling me that you can't fight against a messed-up ghost that's almost three hundred years old?"

Drummond-Stanton bent forward and flexed his muscles like a television wrestler. Then he did something that terrified Max. He stepped forward.

Max quickly understood his mistake. Drummond-Stanton was not actually tethered to the stone at ten feet. He merely wanted to stay that close to the thing. But the more annoying Max had been, the more motivation Drummond-Stanton had to go further out. If he thought at all, that creature must have thought it could swat Max dead and then return to its stone.

But like a toddler learning to break free from its mother, Drummond-Stanton took one look back to make sure his stone was still there. Only it wasn't. Max and Drummond-Stanton both saw Sandra hustling up the path, and they both knew she carried the stone.

Drummond-Stanton shrieked — a far worse sound than he had yet to make — and chased after her. Max tailed behind. Every step the giant made required Max to take three just to keep pace. He pressed harder, gaining ground and ignoring the constant pains in his lungs. As he drew near, he jumped forward, clasping the tattered remains of Drummond-Stanton's coat.

The dead beast reached down, latched onto Max's leg, and hurled him into the path ahead. Straining for breath, Max saw Drummond-Stanton charging forward. Without giving himself time to reconsider, he rolled into Drummond-Stanton's legs, toppling the giant like a sawed redwood.

Stumbling to his feet, Max edged around Drummond-Stanton before jogging up the path. He knew Drummond-Stanton would be on his tail soon enough, but until that moment, he focused on the next step, and the next, and the next.

When he limped out of the woods, he saw Sandra crossing the street. He never stopped moving. Pushing through — that was the way. That was always the way.

Though it seemed to take an hour, Max reached the Allen House in less than five minutes. Sandra stood at the side of the house and yanked on the root cellar door. It would not budge. When she saw Max, she rushed over.

"I was worried you wouldn't —"

"I'm fine. Beaten as all hell, but I'm fine."

She kissed him. "I can't get the door open."

He rattled the old door's handle. Maybe on another day, he could have succeeded. But with the abuse his body had suffered, he lacked the strength to force open the lock.

"Together, then," Sandra said, bending next to him to grab the handle.

When she lowered her body, Max saw Drummond-Stanton tearing up the ground as he stampeded toward them. Operating on instinct, Max reached under Sandra's arms and lifted her backwards. They collapsed on the grass as Drummond-Stanton punched where they had just been. The momentum of his body and the force of his strike smashed through the root cellar door. He toppled down the ladder leading below.

"Hurry," Sandra said, back on her feet.

Max got in front of her, flicked on his cellphone light, and dropped into the cellar. Despite the erratic flickering from his damaged cellphone, he saw enough. To the left of the ladder, he spotted a potato barrel. Beams overhead from the floor of the house poked through the dirt. The walls and floor were unfinished — wooden framework and plenty of red clay. It smelled damp, and the temperature dropped at least ten degrees from the surface.

Ahead, Drummond-Stanton stood bent in the cramped space. He swiped at Max but more for the point of making a threat than actually attacking — not enough room for a giant to maneuver.

As Sandra stepped down the ladder, Max said, "Go over by the barrel. How long will your spell take?"

"I don't know. I've never done it before."

"You said it was a fast spell."

"Looks like it is. We'll see."

"Fine, fine. Get started. Do you need the stone?"

She paused. "Um, that's one thing I forgot to mention. The stone kind of has to be in the hands of the target."

Max's body slumped against the ladder. With a sigh, he put out his hand and she placed the stone in his palm. He did not welcome the heat radiating from it. Drummond-Stanton saw the stone and moved for it, but his head smacked into a beam.

"Easy there, big guy," Max said. "I know you want this. I'm going to give it to you. Okay? Only thing is, I have a feeling that if I just hand it to you, you're going to bolt for the door and I'll never see you again. We can't have that."

A low lion growl rumbled from Drummond-Stanton's throat.

Sandra struck a match and the light flickered around the small cellar. Bits of white peeked through the red clay walls. Bone?

"Hey, Stanton." Max held the stone in front of him like a weapon. "Since you're doing such a good job of blocking Drummond from talking, maybe you're the one I should try speaking with. What do you think? Can you hear me?"

Drummond-Stanton lowered its head, shuffled forward, and swiped for the stone. Max yanked it out of reach. The creature yelped in frustration.

While Sandra murmured her spell and drew circles with a lit candle, Max pointed to the wall. "See that, Stanton? That's bone. Might be yours."

Drummond-Stanton followed Max's finger to the wall.

"That's right. Probably not that one — you'd be going nuts for it, if it was — but I'm sure we'll find other bones in these walls. Maybe even the floor. You've got to be here somewhere." Max stepped nearer. "You think maybe we can stop fighting and help you find your remains?"

But Max had moved too close. Drummond-Stanton lashed out, catching Max in the side. Max bowled over to the wall, his head smacking the hard clay. The stone popped from his hands and onto the floor.

For a second, neither he nor Drummond-Stanton moved. They both stared at it in shock. But then Drummond-Stanton lunged forward as Max dropped down on top of the stone. Curling into a ball, Max clutched the warm rock against his stomach. And the beating began.

Like a Neanderthal, Drummond-Stanton pounded Max with his fists. He shouted and punched, shouted and kicked, and shouted more. The creature's enormous sound doubled in the confined space, but Max could not cover his ears without letting go of the stone. He scrunched his shoulders, but that did nothing to help.

"Max," Sandra cried. "I'm ready. Give him the stone."

When Max rolled onto his back to hand the stone, Drummond-Stanton scooped him up and tossed him into the wall. Max, the stone, and a loosened bone piled onto the floor.

Dazed, Max used the wall to get back on his feet. He steadied himself and looked for the stone. No need. Drummond-Stanton had it, and he headed for the ladder.

"Not yet, big guy," Max said, wrapping his arms around the creature's waist. He let his body go limp so that his entire weight dragged on Drummond-Stanton.

Sandra held the candle up towards the creature's face. She recited words that meant nothing to Max. Drummond-Stanton pulled back his arm, made a fist, and swung at her.

Before he could finish the strike, however, the stone in his other hand flashed greenish light. He dropped the stone and jumped back, tripping on Max's clinging body, and tumbling to the floor. His legs tangled over Max, pining Max to the dirt.

"Light of ancient wisdom, shine upon us." Sandra picked up the stone and its green light intensified. "Light of ages past, favor us. Unite what was once parted. Bring soul to stone and stone to bone. Let this man find his home."

Like a developed X-ray, the dark wall behind Sandra glowed in three places. Each glow taking on the shape of a human bone — the pelvic bone, a shoulder blade, and a cracked skull. The light from the stone faded as the bones in the wall became more numerous. Soon the entire wall pulsed green with pieces of a skeleton.

Chester Stanton lifted into the air. Max had expected a painful and slow process similar to what had joined Stanton with Drummond, but this proved to be smoother, easier. He simply rose from the joined creature as he had once been — a ghost. Still elongated and shredded by his previous actions of long ago, Stanton drifted toward the glowing wall.

The giant body that kept Max down crumbled. It fell apart like wet sand. As Max sat up, Stanton placed one finger against the wall. The glow brightened, flashed, and went dark. Under the amber light of Sandra's candle, Stanton had gone as well.

"My head hurts." The familiar, gruff voice brought a smile to Max's face.

"Drummond!"

"Shhh! That was, by far, the most unpleasant experience of my life and my death."

In a hush, Max said, "You did good, partner. Stanton's gone."

"What are you talking about? He's right here."

Max looked at Drummond, then Sandra, then the wall. To answer his confused look, Sandra said, "You were able to see Stanton because of the spell that connected him to Drummond and you can see Drummond. That's probably why you saw the other ghosts, too. Because through Drummond and Stanton, you were connected to that visual wavelength."

"But they're separated now. The spell is over." Max got to his feet. "That's okay with me. Seeing Drummond is more than enough." Brushing off bits of wet clay, he added, "Are we done here?"

"I am," Drummond said. "I need a week or two to rest this off."

With his arm over Sandra's shoulder, Max managed to climb out of the cellar and limp toward the road. Drummond disappeared, presumably, into the Other. As they neared the road, a car flashed its lights. They headed toward J and Mrs. Porter, but then Max stopped.

Further down the road, a figure stood under a streetlight — Leon Moore. The large man waved his hand in one short motion before turning away, walking out of sight.

Sandra said, "Guess they wanted to make sure we succeeded."

"I think if we hadn't, he would've come in to clean us all up. And I don't want to know what that would mean."

Patting his side, Sandra said, "Come on. Let's go home."

Chapter 30

THREE DAYS LATER, Max, Sandra, and J took Mrs. Porter to the Piedmont International Airport in Greensboro. While large enough to act as a FedEx hub, the airport had a quaint, small town feel. Amongst the echoing announcements of flight departures, the squeak of luggage wheels, and occasional rumble of a jet taking off, Max hugged his mother and kissed her cheek.

"You sure you have to go?" he said.

Sandra added, "We really would like you to stay longer."

Mrs. Porter ruffled J's head. "No, thank you. It's sweet of you to offer but I have things to get to back home."

J wrapped his arms around her. "They don't say stuff they don't mean. You should stay." When he pulled away, Max caught him surreptitiously dabbing at his eyes.

"Now, Max, you make sure to call me more often," his mother said. "I don't like to always have to track you down. You're here and there and busy, busy, busy. I'm usually at home. So pick up a phone and call your mother."

"Yes, ma'am." He escorted her into the check-in line and motioned for Sandra and J to stand back. Lowering his voice so that only she could here, he said, "I overheard you and J talking the other night."

"Oh?"

"I know you don't have anybody left up there. But we're here, and we'd love for you to stay."

"I doubt that. Your wife and I —"

"It was her idea. Besides, the two of you are getting along much better now."

"I wouldn't say that, but I suppose it's not as bad as it was."

"See that? And if you were here, you'd have J around, too."

"You're a sweet boy," she said and patted his cheek. "I appreciate the offer. Had you made it the first few days after I got here, I would have taken you up on it. But after seeing the life you live — well, the Porter Agency life is a bit too chaotic for me."

Max held his mother's hand as they waited in line. *Chaotic.* In the days since their experiences at the Alamance Battlefield, that was the closest she had come to acknowledging any of the supernatural aspects. She could talk about Wallace and his cult, she could discuss the dangers they faced at the hands of a madman, but nothing more. She refused to mention Drummond, Stanton, witchcraft, or even the inscribed stone. None of it existed to her.

J took it all a bit better. At first chance, he hustled over to PB and recounted everything he had seen. But PB had plausible answers for everything — tricks of the moonlight, the cult had probably drugged him, and an overactive imagination that wanted to impress Max.

By the time they drove to the airport, neither J nor Mrs. Porter believed they had seen a ghost. If his mother had stayed, Max would have worked hard to let her see the reality of his life. She could have made a good asset to the agency. But since she insisted on returning home, he thought it best that she continue to deny the supernatural. It would make her weekly bridge games easier if the other elderly ladies did not have fodder for their sharp tongues.

Max glanced over at Sandra. After all that had happened, her interest in witchcraft had only strengthened. Rather than curling up with a good mystery or a romance novel, she spent most of her nights reading old tomes and dusty volumes of lore or combing through the hardcore witchcraft websites. He knew they benefited from her knowledge, but he could not shake the thought that nothing good would come of this.

"You know," Mrs. Porter said, nudging Max with her shoulder, "there is one thing you could do for me that would make this all much better."

"Sure. What?"

"Get me some grandchildren."

Max started to protest but his mother launched into a verbal diatribe of reasons that Sandra needed to start reproducing. His skin prickled, but a smile crept onto his face. The longer she spoke, the happier he became.

At length, he kissed her head. "I love you, Mom."

"I love you, too, but that's not the point."

He kissed her again. "I got the point. More than you know."

She eyed him for a moment and then peeked over at Sandra and J. Biting her lip, she patted her luggage. In a quiet voice, she said, "I'd have to get my own place."

"What?" Max said.

Louder this time, she said, "If I'm going to live here, I would require my own place. Let's be honest about this — it would never work for me to be under your roof all the time."

Max's gut flipped in an acrobatic mixture of excitement and fear. "But you just said —"

"And I've reconsidered. That boy needs a good parent, somebody who knows what she's doing. Your office could use some help, too. Now, I'm not saying I want to go traipsing around the woods anymore. I meant it — that's too chaotic for me. But I'm sure I can find a way to be useful. If you still want me, that is."

Wrapping his arms around her, he said, "We do. Always."

She hugged him back, and for a fleeting second, Max remembered what it was like to be her little boy. Sniffling, she said, "Then it's settled. When I get back to Michigan, I'll sell the house and get my things together and come down here. You start looking for an apartment for me. Nothing too noisy. Check out the neighbors. I'll call you later and explain the best way to do that."

As she rambled on, Max rocked on his heels and smiled.

"What now?" she said when she noticed his expression.

"Nothing. I'm happy, that's all. I don't know why you changed your mind, but I'm happy."

"No big secret. Like you said, there's nobody up there for me anymore." She glanced at Sandra. "Besides which, how are you two going to have a baby, if I'm not around to make sure it happens? You've had more than enough time on your own to get it done."

Max looked over at Sandra. He wondered if she had heard any of the conversation. The roll of her eyes answered his thoughts. The two of them laughed loud and full.

Afterword

Well, here we are again, at the end of another Max Porter tale. Thank you for taking the journey with me. I know what you're looking for here, though, so I'll get right to it:

Most of the story surrounding the Battle of Alamance is true. The build up to the battle is also true. Governor Tryon and his cronies abused the land distribution system, and Husband and the Regulators fought back. It all culminated in a battle on a small patch of land in the middle of North Carolina.

You can visit the battlefield today and see the various positions people fought from, including Pugh's Rock. They are frighteningly close to each other. The James Allen House that had been moved to the property is still there and you can go step inside the one-room home for a real sense of living conditions of the time.

You'll also be able to find the trails leading back into the woods complete with signage along the trail marking where Tryon's horse fell and other moments. Unless the Parks and Rec Department changes the paths, you should be able to locate the somewhat circular clearing that I used for the midnight rites performed by Wallace. Also, there were, indeed, six men hanged after the battle.

What you won't find is any reference to the three men cursed by the witch Abigail. I made them up. The extra coffins were a fiction from my head, too. Other locations such as the bog garden are real, as is the Green Valley Grill in the O. Henry Hotel. It's delicious, by the way.

Acknowledgements

First off, a big, big thank you to Claudia Ianniciello for her stupendous artwork. After the great work of Duncan Long on the blue books and then Jeff Dekal's equally brilliant work on the red books, Claudia had big shoes to fill. I think she surpassed my expectations, and I look forward to the rest of her work on the green books. Thanks also to Jeremiah DeGennaro of the Alamance Battleground Park. Jeremiah spent quite a bit of time with me, showing me around the battlefield and explaining the details I would come to use for this novel. Of course, any mistakes are mine. I take notes, but sometimes I can't read them all that well. Endless thanks go to my Launch Team for all their support, and in particular, Toni Shepherd and Lisa Gall for helping to catch the typos the editors missed. As always, to Glory and Gabe.

Lastly, my thanks to you, my reader. Every day I'm blessed to write these stories knowing that you are out there, eager to find out what my brain came up with for Max, Sandra, and Drummond. Without you, their lives would never have taken off. In many ways, neither would have mine.

Thank you.

About the Author

Stuart Jaffe is the madman behind *The Max Porter Paranormal Mysteries,* the *Nathan K* thrillers, *The Malja Chronicles, The Bluesman, Founders, Real Magic,* and so much more. He trained in martial arts for over a decade until a knee injury ended that practice. Now, he plays lead guitar in a local blues band, *The Bootleggers,* and enjoys life on a small farm in rural North Carolina. For those who continue to keep count, the animal list is as follows: one dog, two cats, three aquatic turtles, one albino corn snake, seven chickens, and a horse. As best as he's been able to manage, Stuart has made sure that the chickens and the horse do not live in the house.

www.ingramcontent.com/pod-product-compliance
Lightning Source LLC
Chambersburg PA
CBHW030519310726
48979CB00010B/1734/J

* 9 7 8 1 9 6 3 5 1 7 0 0 2 *